MARTIN
BUTTERFIELD

MARTIN
BUTTERFIELD

By John Burgan

Jacket drawing by
Norman Guthrie Rudolph

jB91m

THE JOHN C. WINSTON COMPANY

PHILADELPHIA • TORONTO

TO JOE AND IRENE

OTHER BOOKS BY JOHN BURGAN

Two Per Cent Fear

Long Discovery

This novel was based on the short story "The Show-Off," which originally appeared in *The Saturday Evening Post*.

CONTENTS

CHAPTER 1

Boy of Promise

MARTIN BUTTERFIELD sat uneasily at the supper table between his father and mother on the evening of the last day of school in Fern Township.

He bent his dark, close-clipped head over his mashed potatoes and ate intently while his final report card was being scrutinized by Mr. Butterfield. From time to time he eyed his father's ominously bridged black brows and his mother's troubled, gentle face.

Mentally, he resolved to do better when he started fifth grade next autumn.

He was certainly glad, in this emergency, that he had some good news to impart. However, he decided to withhold it until his elders had digested all the bad news contained in his report card.

He did not, it developed, have long to wait.

Suddenly looking up from the card to his sole heir, Mr. Butterfield spoke in the voice he reserved for times of catastrophe.

"With marks as bad as these, Martin," Mr. Butterfield

said, "what do you think is going to happen to you when you grow up?"

Martin was gratified that he had saved the best until last.

"Today at closing exercises," he informed his father, "the fourth grade voted me the Boy Most Likely to Succeed in Life."

It was a wonderfully timed blow.

Mr. Butterfield, who was not only the calmest trial lawyer in Fern Township but, more admirably yet, the canniest rabbit hunter, keenest beagle handler, and most nerveless rifle marksman, let his fork clatter to his plate.

"What?" Mr. Butterfield gasped.

Martin reached into his shirt pocket.

"Here is the certificate Miss Gillis gave me," Martin said, beaming first at his father and then at his mother, thus equally dividing the honor he had shed upon them at school.

There was no denying the paper's authenticity. Mr. Butterfield had seen plenty of the fourth-grade teacher's Palmer Method handwriting in connection with less cheering forecasts for Martin's future.

"How did this happen?" Mr. Butterfield murmured incredulously, passing the document to his wife.

"The other pupils voted for me," Martin said benignly. "We had voting for lots of things—Best Scholar, Best Scientist—just lots of things."

"Well, bless my soul!" was Mr. Butterfield's response.

"Why, Martin, how nice!" said Mrs. Butterfield. She leaned over and kissed her offspring. "Who else got certificates?"

Martin reflected. Dangerous ground, this.

"Georgianna Semple was the Best Scholar," he said. "Shorty Dunston was Best Scientist . . ."

"Didn't Sparky Roberts get anything?" Mr. Butterfield asked.

2

Sparky Roberts was a tall, blond ten-year-old who not only had big muscles but was also Martin's best friend.

"Yes," Martin replied, "Sparky was voted the Most Athletic Boy."

Martin was gratified that this seemed to end the subject of Sparky Roberts.

In fact, Martin preferred to forget Sparky Roberts altogether for the time being, because Sparky was not disassociated from Martin's own honor. The truth was that Martin had been elected to the Fourth Grade Hall of Fame by an old and honored electioneering technique.

He had promised Sparky a gift in return for Sparky's support. And Sparky, the Most Athletic Boy, had promised the rest of the male element of fourth grade something prospectively less entrancing if they did not vote for Martin.

Somehow, Martin felt now that suppertime was not exactly the right moment to inform Mr. Butterfield that Sparky Roberts expected shortly to receive one of Mr. Butterfield's prize beagle puppies.

This was the gift that Martin had promised.

The son now scrutinized his father closely. His father returned the gaze with clearly blossoming parental pride.

Mr. Butterfield gave Martin a quarter.

This financial boon enabled Martin to spend the evening with Messrs. Gene Autry, Roy Rogers, Champion and Trigger, far removed from the problems of his own social and political world.

But the world never stays in place very long. By the next morning, it began—in the strong young person of Sparky Roberts—to close inexorably upon Martin Butterfield.

Sparky was sitting in the Butterfield kitchen when Martin came downstairs, and he waited while Martin breakfasted. Then the two friends sallied out the back door, a pair of small boys in the blissful springtime of life when the sky is cloudless and the future golden.

No sooner had they reached the grove of sunlit maples near the Butterfield beagle kennels, however, than Sparky Roberts clouded the sky and tarnished the gold.

"Let's go and look at the puppies," he suggested.

"How about going swimming first?" Martin countered.

"You better not try to welsh on that puppy," Sparky advised.

"Who's welshing?" inquired Martin.

"I'll tell everybody how you got elected."

"We'll take just one peek at the puppies," Martin conceded miserably.

The old beagle came down the pen run with her seven fat children tumbling brightly about her feet.

The two boys did not deal in platitudes canine.

"Them puppies are big enough to leave their mother now," Sparky Roberts said.

"How'd you like it if somebody took you away from your mother?" Martin inquired with sentiment.

"When do I get my puppy?" Sparky asked flatly and threateningly.

"When the puppies are ready," Martin replied.

"How long?" Sparky inquired.

"Tomorrow," Martin said abruptly, tomorrow being a highly theoretical and hypothetical quantity to persons ten years old.

"Cross your fingers!" Sparky demanded.

Martin held up the traditional symbol of good faith.

"Both hands!"

Martin doubled the ante.

"Now cross your heart!"

Martin solemnly crossed his crossed fingers in a third cross over his diaphragm.

4

Sparky Roberts stooped and picked up a puppy and felt it carefully.

"I hope you ain't lying," he said, putting the pup down. "Now let's go swimming in Lick Creek."

In this gentle mood, the two friends went around the rear of the stable and then took off, cross lots, toward Lick Creek Highway at the lower end of the township. It is not unlikely that they would have suspended all argument in favor of some other pursuit if they had not reached the highway at the end of Lick Creek Bridge at a most opportune moment for masculine competitive sports.

Under a beech tree by the road, resting from hiking, were a grown lady and twelve little girls—the annual picnic of the Junior Girls' Sunday-School Class of the First Presbyterian Church. Martin and Sparky inspected this phenomenon briefly but with approximately the same amount of interest they would have shown to a herd of rhinoceros grazing in Fern Township.

"What's that?" Sparky Roberts snorted disgustedly.

"Some old girls," Martin said with equal distaste.

"What do they think they're doing?"

"Going on some old picnic, I guess."

It was only a coincidence that just in front of the beech tree Martin Butterfield happened to turn a handspring. Sparky duplicated the feat and embellished it with an afterpiece of tumbling, as if he had been planning this very action all morning.

"You think that's anything?" Martin asked.

Thereupon the road that led up to the high steel structure of Lick Creek Bridge became a stage. Martin reared up on his hands and walked ten paces, feet straight up in the air. But the ten paces, instead of carrying him toward the bridge, only took him in a circle which ended right in front of the beech tree. There was an audible stir under the tree.

"Anybody can walk on their hands," Sparky Roberts said.

Some of the little girls were equally ungrateful. "Boys," loudly observed Georgianna Semple, the Best Scholar in fourth grade, "are such big show-offs."

Martin found reason to move away from the tree and pick up a well-shaped throwing stone, with which he expertly hit the top girder of Lick Creek Bridge. Sparky Roberts, without so much as a word, picked up a larger stone and made a louder ding on the high metal.

Martin Butterfield was thoroughly surfeited with his bosom friend, Sparky Roberts. He felt the cornered hero's need for the devastating blow—the quick jujutsu punch, the grand-slam home run, the last-minute touchdown gallop.

Before he considered the inevitable result of braggadocio, Martin looked up at the steel altitude of Lick Creek Bridge.

"I'm not afraid to climb up on top of the bridge," he announced.

Now it happens that the cantilever superstructure of Lick Creek Highway Bridge is high. Nobody was more aware of that fact than Martin, standing there in the sunny road after making his boast. Rising at a forty-five-degree angle, the slanting bridgehead girders seemed to reach the blue June heavens.

"Why don't you go up, then?" Sparky inquired mildly.

Martin hastily reefed some of his untimely sail. "I just don't want to," he replied truthfully.

"Just don't want to!" Sparky mimicked.

Sparky's sarcasm rocked the gentle morning air, and more especially it rocked the befrocked, bepinafored and beslacked audience under the tree.

"I'll go up if you go up," Martin offered meekly.

"Phooey to you," Sparky Roberts replied. "You said —"

Martin Butterfield had to make a dreadful decision. He stood in the road kicking at pebbles thoughtfully. Sheer, cruel necessity was working the miracle of an idea in the fertile brain of the Boy Most Likely to Succeed; to wit: *If I have to do this awful thing, I might as well fix Sparky Roberts good.* Martin just stood there doubtfully. And his hesitation had the desired effect.

"You ain't gonna do it!" Sparky jeered confidently. "You're scared!"

"Wanna bet?" Martin retorted.

"The whole world!"

"Okay, I'll bet that beagle puppy I owe you."

Sparky Roberts saw the trick too late.

"You ain't gonna do it," he said half-questioningly.

"It's a bet," Martin said, with more firmness than he felt.

After all, this wasn't just a question of showing a bunch of girls what you could do; a dog was at stake.

Before Sparky Roberts could reconsider the bet, Martin walked with condemned-man bravado to the base of the bridge truss and clambered up on the slanting steel catwalk of the bridge.

Martin heard the commotion under the beech tree, but he concentrated all his attention on the shining rivets in the steel beam, up which he crawled like a cautious monkey. In the torture of doing a thing that scared and sobered him, Martin mentally noted a new axiom of personal conduct: Never again trade your father's dogs for anything without first asking your father. It was only when Martin sank to this bitter nadir of regret that he made a heart-warming discovery. Climbing up a bridge wasn't so fearful as he had imagined it would be.

This inoculation of confidence propelled him up the last few feet of the great superstructure in a final, wonderful spurt. When the upper filigree of steel girders, turnbuckles

7

and crosspieces finally spread out levelly before him and the countryside fell away below, Martin felt that it was pretty easy to be a hero if you were brave enough.

Only then did he deign to glance down on the less altitudinous world of the road below. What he saw down there filled him with a delight that sparkled inside him like white diamonds. The bridge floor directly beneath him was occupied not only by the upturned face of Sparky Roberts but also by a small pond of faces belonging to the Junior Girls' Sunday-School Class of the First Presbyterian Church.

It is a well-known fact that a hero's first taste of public attention sometimes develops a ravening appetite for further adulation. It was even thus with Martin Butterfield as he sat there looking down from his hot steel perch high over the world.

Forgotten was his victory over Sparky Roberts. Faded was the fact that he had "saved" one of his father's beagle puppies. Gone was the knowledge that he had got himself out of a developing catastrophe as concerned his father. Martin could be stirred now only by the vision of newer and greater worlds to conquer.

He decided to stand up erect on the bridge. Taking a deep breath, he twisted around on the narrow girder and pulled one foot under him. With a final, quick balancing motion he stood up, a lone small figure standing like a rod against the blue morning sky.

And that was when the inevitable happened. Somehow, in a manner he could not afterwards recall, the Boy Most Likely to Succeed in Life almost became the Boy Most Likely to Wind Up in the Hospital. Martin slipped.

There was a gaspy shriek from fourteen throats below as he lost his footing and plummeted down toward the floor of the bridge. But Martin did not go far. By some trick of posture, his feet stayed together, and he shot straight into a small hole between girders and turnbuckles, coming to an abrupt halt at his waistline.

When the screams had risen and died on the summer air, Martin was as firmly in place as a nickel in a slot. His head stuck out above the girders and his feet flapped in the breeze below. By the time that tears would normally have welled, he found himself clasped in a steel embrace from which it was impossible to fall or get out. Silently Martin looked down on the faces looking up.

"Jumpin' jiminy!" Sparky Roberts, loser of a beagle in the deal, gasped.

At this point the lady Sunday-school teacher took over. "Run and get the fire department!" she cried.

It was a thought of such brilliance that a boy could never have expected it from a grown-up lady. The fire department! Martin felt vaguely sorry for such diminished heroes as Joe DiMaggio and General MacArthur.

By the time the township's lone fire truck arrived, there were the makings of a township mass meeting on the bridge-head. Highway traffic halted at the bridge and people came from nowhere.

Martin Butterfield, meanwhile, had sobered considerably from his previous elation—not without reason. His father was a member of the volunteer fire department. His father was a lawyer who liked to ask questions. His father might ask, "How did you happen to decide to go up there?" Maybe his father would yet find out that behind the bridge climbing was a beagle puppy, and behind the beagle puppy, the election of the Boy Most Likely to Succeed.

Martin was the first, naturally, to see the fire truck coming. He was also the first to note Mr. Butterfield desperately clinging to the fire truck right beside Sparky Roberts.

The red vehicle roared toward the bridge amid scattering spectators, and even before it had stopped, Martin heard his father's voice: "Martin! Are you all right?"

Strangely, Mr. Butterfield was not using the tone which usually preceded the application of the razor strap to Martin's pants. He seemed to be worried, even kindly, as regarded Martin.

"I'm okay, Dad!" Martin shouted down into his father's upturned face.

The fire chief, who was Mr. Buckmaster the grocer in disguise, erected the ladder. In a moment he and Mr. Butterfield were swarming over Martin on top of the bridge.

Martin felt his father's hands go over him, searching his bones and muscles for damage.

"You're all right, son?" Again the kind voice.

Meanwhile it took Mr. Buckmaster only a moment to discover that Martin was in danger of taking up permanent residence atop the bridge.

"He's sure stuck, George," said Mr. Buckmaster to Mr. Butterfield.

Martin was nothing if not helpful. "You could get a torch and burn off some of the steel," he suggested. What a fine scene that would make!

"Well . . ." said Mr. Buckmaster.

Martin's ideas were by no means exhausted. "Why don't you pull me by the feet?" he inquired. He could drop into a life net, just like the movies.

Mr. Butterfield silently probed around Martin's waist with a big forefinger, and presently reached Martin's belt buckle.

"Here's the trouble, Buck," he said to the fire chief. "His belt buckle is stuck under the girder."

Mr. Buckmaster felt the buckle too.

The chief reflected a moment. "We could reach up from the ladder underneath," he said, "and unfasten it."

"That ought to do it," Mr. Butterfield agreed.

Martin took no further part in these discussions. It did not matter what they did now, so long as the crowd below continued to grow. His mother was nowhere in sight yet, however, and that was a pang. He felt that she ought not to be deprived of his moment of glory. Occasionally he waved to a favored acquaintance and nodded from time to time at good old Sparky, his friend, who was now pale green with envy, Martin imagined.

It was not until Martin felt his belt buckle being manipulated by a fireman from beneath the girder that he had an uneasy thought. In a moment this tiny worry blossomed into a terrible fear that was justified in every respect.

Once his belt buckle was unfastened, Martin felt the strong hands of his father and Mr. Buckmaster lift him skyward. Martin sailed right out of the hole—and also right out of his pants, which dropped limply in the other direction to the floor of the bridge. A great roar swelled from below. There, in broad daylight, before the Junior Girls and the assembled township, Martin was dangled affectionately by his father. The famous hero was wearing red polka-dotted underwear.

The trip down the ladder on his father's shoulder was a nightmare in which Martin saw and heard nothing. Desperately, he searched the ground as his father climbed down and, when set on his feet, he darted for the pants like a sand crab for its burrow.

Deaf with anguish and blind with embarrassment, Martin had already drawn them on and was fastening the offending belt buckle when he noted something interesting in the crowd's manner. They were still happily cheering his rescue. He was still a hero.

It was stunning to listen to the uproar.

"Thank heaven for that!" It was his father.

"I don't know how he did it, but it sure caused some excitement!" That was Mr. Buckmaster, the fire chief.

"Everybody in town's here!" That was the lady Sunday-school teacher.

Thus Martin made one of the discoveries that constitute growing up: What a hero does—like getting stuck on top of a bridge—is more important than how he gets out of it —like losing his trousers publicly.

Martin stood among the forest of tall adults until he felt his father sweep him up impulsively. Mr. Butterfield carried him like a baby and set him up on the highest coil of fire hose on the truck, a king on his throne. While the people clapped, Mr. Butterfield climbed in beside his son, and Mr. Buckmaster mounted the driver's seat.

Martin looked down again upon his audience. He smiled at Georgianna Semple, and she actually smiled back. He looked for Sparky Roberts, but could not immediately find him.

Sparky's sad, envious eyes were too close to him, peering right over the side of the truck.

Seeing him at last, Martin felt the compassion of the great for the obscure.

"Dad," he said, "can Sparky ride on the truck too?"

Mr. Butterfield swooped down and hauled the secondary hero aboard, seating him next to Martin on the high coil of hose, really more honor than Martin had intended for Sparky.

"Good old Sparky," Mr. Butterfield said. "Good boy!"

Sparky hung his head modestly as the truck engine roared to life.

Martin looked at his pal suspiciously. Was there a threat in Sparky's eye? Would Sparky yet go and tell everybody about the beagle puppy deal?

Martin snuggled up to his father. "Sparky sure got the

12

fire department quick, didn't he?" Martin reminded Mr. Butterfield.

"We owe Sparky a great deal," said Mr. Butterfield with feeling.

With that remark, Mr. Butterfield laid himself wide open to the very suggestion that Martin had in mind. Martin knew how to settle that debt.

"Why don't we give Sparky a beagle puppy, huh?" he said.

Martin was glad to observe that the threat in Sparky's eye died then and there.

"I think it could be arranged," Mr. Butterfield said, although he had not had any previous plans for such a large token of appreciation. "Would you like that, Sparky?"

"It would be nice," Sparky said in a small ten-year-old voice, as the truck moved out of the crowd.

Only Martin Butterfield saw Sparky cross his fingers—both hands—and make a little X across his heart. As the truck rolled off, the boys laced comradely arms about each other's shoulders.

Mr. Butterfield looked down upon his son with secret pride in the boy's daring and with open admiration of his sense of loyalty to a friend. That kind of boy would go far in life. It hurt Mr. Butterfield's conscience a little that he had not perceived this conspicuous truth before Martin's fourth-grade comrades had proclaimed it to the whole world.

CHAPTER 2

Trial by Water

THERE is an illusion, as wrong as it is widespread, that heroism has a natural companion in modesty. The plain fact is, as a glance at any military man's rows of clamoring ribbons will tell you, that heroes like recognition.

On the day after his exploit at Lick Creek Bridge, Martin Butterfield arose early in order that his day of public acclaim might be long. The son and heir of the Butterfield estate arrived at the breakfast table simultaneously with his father.

While Mrs. Butterfield put another egg into the boiling water on the stove for this added starter, Mr. Butterfield inspected his offspring speculatively.

"How are you this fine morning, Martin?" he inquired.

"I'm fine, sir," replied Martin with a stiff courtesy altogether foreign to him.

"You're certainly up early enough," Mr. Butterfield said.

"A person doesn't want to sleep all his life away, I guess," Martin replied.

Mr. Butterfield drank deeply of his scorchingly hot coffee. A heroic son might just possibly be more than he could bear, he thought.

He looked at his wife searchingly. With a movement of her eyelashes she discouraged an impending bit of parental sarcasm; Mr. Butterfield proceeded silently into action against a pair of soft-boiled eggs.

As Mrs. Butterfield sat down, steps sounded on the back porch and the Butterfield family looked up to greet Sparky Roberts.

"Another early riser," Mr. Butterfield remarked. "Come in, Sparky," he called.

"Hi!" Martin said.

"Hi!" replied his friend, sidling to a chair.

He sure can't wait to get that dog, Martin thought.

"I'll fix you up with your puppy right after breakfast," Mr. Butterfield said.

"Okay," Sparky replied meekly.

After breakfast, Martin, Sparky and Mr. Butterfield repaired to the dog kennel where Mr. Butterfield selected a small and—he hoped—not particularly promising beagle pup from the litter and turned the animal over to Sparky.

"You take good care of him, Sparky," he said, "or I'll come around and take him back."

He bade the boys good-by and started for the house. On the way up the rear steps, just as Martin and Sparky were slipping out the back gate, Mr. Butterfield halted.

"Martin," he called, "you better give this lawn a good going-over with the lawn mower today."

Martin paused. He looked at Sparky. Sparky returned the look.

"Okay," Martin said mildly.

It should not be construed that this reply meant either (a) that Martin agreed the lawn ought to be mowed; or (b) that he intended to mow it. "Okay," as used in this sense, was merely a boy's way of closing immediately an odious subject of discussion.

Martin and Sparky hung on the back gate for a minute inspecting the puppy, whose shivering liquid black-and-white form lay in Sparky's hands.

"How can we get a doghouse built if you have to cut the grass?" Sparky asked.

"I got all day," Martin said.

"What kind of doghouse should we build?" Sparky inquired.

Martin hung on the gate and reflected. He felt expansive this morning. He and Sparky Roberts would build the biggest doghouse ever seen in Fern Township. Not only the biggest, but the best.

That they had no materials for such a venture at the moment troubled Martin not at all.

He and Sparky would go downtown instantly and scrounge some old packing boxes. This part of the doghouse-building appealed immensely to Martin, because it would take him into the public eye where the people of the town could see the brave figure who had climbed up Lick Creek Bridge and had come home in the fire truck. Martin could hear his imagined admirers' questions before the questions were asked:

Were you scared up there? . . . What made you want to do that? . . . What if you had fallen into the creek, Marty? . . .

He would be careless in his answers . . . It wasn't anything . . . Anybody could do it if he had nerve enough. . . .

"Let's go downtown and get the lumber," Martin said.

Thus was the beginning of a summer morning happily spent by Martin Butterfield. If people seemed a little less interested in his feat than Martin had imagined they might, he made up for it by telling them a little more about it than he had anticipated he would.

The collecting of boxes and of reluctant tribute was a time-consuming occupation. Not only had the morning fled, but the first fine flame of doghouse-building enthusiasm had burned low indeed by noon.

High noon found the beagle puppy sleeping in a wooden grocery box in the cellar of the Roberts home, a pile of grocery boxes stacked in the Roberts back yard, and the dog's two closest friends some blocks distant, reclining on an old car seat in the cool shadows of the old Butterfield barn.

"When you going to mow the lawn, like your father said?" Sparky Roberts inquired of the figure crowded against the wall beside him.

"That's for me to know and you to find out," Martin replied while he stared dimly at the ceiling. He was a little disappointed in the day so far, and he calculated coolly the possibilities of the afternoon that yet lay before him.

He never reached the full flower of a solution to these calculations because the clock on the firehouse struck twelve and the voice of Mrs. Butterfield floated sweetly out on the quiet summer air.

"Martin! Lunch time!"

Sparky Roberts twitched one foot. Martin did not move.

"You hear that, Martin?"

"Hear what?"

"Your mother callin' you."

"Oh!"

Having established some indefinite principle of superiority by letting Sparky call this fact to his attention, Martin wriggled enough to shove Sparky off the old car seat on to the loft floor.

"Hey, quit being so fresh or—" Sparky began.

17

Mrs. Butterfield's voice again penetrated the cool old barn.

"Martin! You come right now!"

Martin forestalled any possibility of physical conflict with Sparky by drowning him and his threat out.

"I'm comin'," he replied in a voice that pierced the barn roof.

"I think I'll go swimmin' this afternoon," Sparky said with as cruel a casualness as he could muster, "while you're mowing the lawn."

Martin studied his friend. "Come around," he said. "Maybe I'll go with you."

Martin's lunch that noon consisted of one yellow and two green vegetables, a slice of bacon, a glass of milk, an admonition to get busy with the lawn mower, and the sudden intelligence that Mrs. Butterfield was going to be away from the house for the afternoon. It was club day.

Martin ate with good appetite and washed the luncheon dishes while his mother finished dressing. He hung up the towel as she left.

When Sparky rejoined him, he had already rolled the lawn mower from the barn to the lawn on the shady side of the house, where he lay down in the grass to study some fleecy white clouds in the deep blue sky.

"You sure work fast," Sparky commented, looking down upon the unshorn grass and the recumbent form.

"Why don't you help me?" Martin inquired in a most friendly fashion. "If you do, I'll go swimming with you."

This proffered bargain caused Sparky to raise his muzzle like a defiant young colt and neigh derisively.

"Remember, I gave you a dog . . ." Martin said.

Sparky was only beginning to respond with proper gratitude to this challenge when a shout came over the front hedge from the street.

18

"Hey, Martin!"

The voice was an imperious one, and it commanded the instant attention, even the respect, of both Martin and Sparky.

It belonged, as any boy in the fourth or fifth grade could readily have stated, to the acknowledged leader of all boys in Fern Township in or below the fifth grade.

"Red Spingarn!" whispered Sparky Roberts, with an awe appropriate to a visit from so prominent a citizen. As will be understood, Red Spingarn did not conduct visitations upon lesser fry in the town as a rule; instead, they waited upon Master Spingarn's pleasure.

As Martin sat up in the grass, a wonderful feeling suddenly suffused him. The recognition he had sought with mixed results this morning was now coming voluntarily to him. Martin got slowly to his feet as Red Spingarn came around the hedge and into full view, followed by several lesser lights in the junior community.

"Hi," Martin said.

Red Spingarn looked at him and then looked at Sparky Roberts with a trace of that detachment which set him apart. At first glance, it was hard to see by what scale of measurement Red Spingarn loomed so important in the lives of so many.

He was a thin, hard youngster, only a trifle taller than his fellows. His hair was a flaming auburn, and it capped a face that was at once bland and sure of itself. In his confident, graceful, animal motion there was a clue to his prominent position in the world of fourth- and fifth-graders. Beside Red Spingarn, even an athletic figure such as Sparky Roberts looked a trifle awkward and indecisive.

Martin viewed the oncoming figure with that mixture of awe, timidity and admiration that is a boy's fullest measure of tribute to another.

He hardly noticed the others in the Spingarn party—Jim Douglas, Johnny Farnsworth, Shorty Dunston and Mack Potter—although the appearance of any of them would have been greeted earlier in the day with a certain measured gratitude for homage rendered.

For Martin was very confident that the honor being paid him was not unconnected with his Lick Creek Bridge feat.

In a way, he was right.

"What you doin'?" Red Spingarn inquired, plucking a blade of grass to chew contemplatively.

"Just mowing the grass," Martin replied.

Red Spingarn inspected the grass for a moment. "Doggone poor job you're doin'," he said, turning to his party and immediately receiving the tribute of raucous laughter that such wit demanded.

Martin shuffled from one foot to the other, unsure of himself in the presence of such company.

Red looked down from the infinitesimally slight elevation in height he enjoyed over Martin. Now was the moment, Martin knew.

"What's that people are saying about you on the bridge?" Red inquired.

Martin managed a look that was almost genuinely modest. "It wasn't anything," he said.

Red chewed on the blade and his confident young face eyed Martin objectively.

"Who said it was?" he returned.

The sudden shift of ground beneath Martin caught him unprepared.

"Well—nobody," he replied.

"Anybody could get stuck on a bridge—especially if he had fly paper on his britches," said Red.

The chorus behind him thought this witticism so well

aimed that two members had to roll in the grass in order to express their appreciation fully.

At this point, Sparky Roberts came cautiously to Martin's defense.

"Martin didn't need any fly paper," he said.

Red Spingarn wheeled with a speed that was a familiar threat to the welfare of all small citizens in Fern Township.

"Another county heard from!" he said.

The county reporting subsided with as much immediacy as it had first intruded itself on the conversation.

There was a silence beside the Butterfield house. Red Spingarn threw away his blade of grass and then, looking at Martin as if to remind himself of the unimportant mission that had brought him there, he issued an invitation that was so careless in tone and manner that Martin understood it instantly as both a challenge and a command.

"Wanna go swimming, maybe, Martin?" Red asked.

Martin did not even glance toward the lawn mower.

"Sparky and I was just goin'," he said carelessly. "Sure we'll go."

Sparky Roberts, however, developed another view. He understood the situation perfectly without drawings and without text, and he saw no compelling reason why he should be involved in risks not of his own making.

"I have to go home," he said, "and work on my doghouse."

And Sparky *was* at home and he *was* working on his doghouse by the time the swimming party arrived on the boulder-fringed bank of the swimming hole in Lick Creek a mile or so below the town.

In the thirty minutes consumed by the hike to the swimming hole, the sentiment of the party had crystallized and hardened to a remarkable degree and in a direction that left Martin Butterfield thinking rather wistfully of the pleasures of lawn mowing at home.

The hero of Lick Creek Bridge was being challenged from every conceivable direction, and Red Spingarn was picking the medium in which all challenges would be decided; namely, the water of the swimming hole where, it was a miserable fact, Red Spingarn had long held undisputed sway as the best swimmer in the township.

The swimming hole among the big gray rocks was a purely male enterprise, so swimmers did not suffer the confinement of bathing suits. A bathing suit, in fact, would have been worn at considerable risk to the wearer.

The boys undressed and placed their clothing in tight bundles well back from the bank, in the not unreasonable expectation that there was going to be almost as much of Lick Creek splashed on the bank as remained in the stream bed.

Red Spingarn did not postpone for more than a fleeting minute his plan for reducing the stature of Martin Butterfield.

It should be understood that there was no spirit of competition in this operation; rather, it was the readily comprehensible and businesslike desire of a leader to put his house in order and his inferiors where they belonged.

Martin Butterfield understood this without even thinking about it. He also understood that he was to play out his rôle to the bitter end if he were to retain a few shreds of respect among the fourth- and fifth-grade communities.

He squared his small brown shoulders resolutely for a moment on the bank of the creek, wondering remorsefully whether it had been wise for a hero to seek so much public recognition so quickly. Martin Butterfield, like most other heroes, had a deep desire to live to enjoy the fruits of his feat.

He plunged into the roiled brown pool of the sluggish creek and came to the surface, blowing through his mouth and nose and snapping his head like a wet dog. The water had not completely cleared from his ears when he heard Red Spingarn announce the beginning of festivities.

"Let's see Martin life-save a drowning man!" Red shouted.

Promptly, Red suited action to word. His long, loose arms clamped Martin so firmly around the gullet that the hero of the bridge would have found it impossible to expire by drowning for the simple reason that he could not inhale the creekful of water in which he suddenly found himself immersed.

Martin acted with a valor that would have done credit to any life guard trying to free himself from his victim. Meanwhile, the drowning man remained directly above both Martin and the surface of the water, loudly reporting on Martin's progress to his audience.

The unequal contest was only concluded when Martin's desperation reached a pitch sufficiently high for him to sink his teeth into one of Red Spingarn's calves, thereby giving Red an interest that took his mind off the life-saving lesson.

Martin came weakly to the surface just in time to fill his bursting lungs with cold, fresh air and suffer the inevitable result of leaving his toothmarks in Red Spingarn's leg.

Through the curtain of water and spray that filled his eyes, nose, mouth, and ears Martin saw, felt, and heard a pair of strong hands fall upon his head and send him beneath the surface again.

In that desperate moment of onslaught, Martin learned the lesson of courage that belongs to the man who has no more to lose by fighting.

He aimed a swift, hard kick—born of some unsuspected final pool of energy—into Red Spingarn's stomach.

He felt his enemy retreat. Still under water, Martin turned and swam, with what he was uncomfortably certain was his last physical action on this terrestrial sphere, around the great rocks that fringed the swimming hole to a concealed niche, finally coming up for air and silently hoping that he would not instantly be located.

On the other side of the rock there was only desultory shouting now.

"We'll fix that smart aleck," he heard Red Spingarn say.

Then he heard the splashing of water as the boys went out on the bank.

Then nothing.

He wondered what plot was forming to fall upon him now. The water felt cold in the shadow of the rocks. But he was too weary to worry about that. In fact, he was too weary to worry about anything.

When he had regained enough wind to consider the affairs of the world and especially his own problematical position therein, the silence on the other side of the rock had deepened.

Martin restrained a questioning impulse. Curiosity on his part now was precisely what Red Spingarn might be laying a trap for.

Martin remained quietly where he was. But he was to learn, as many a more valiant one has learned before him, that suspense is sometimes so hard to bear that action seems preferable.

After what seemed two hours—but was actually less than five minutes—Martin swam cautiously out of his haven and back into full view of the river bank, stoically ready for whatever unmerciful fortune awaited him.

He was all the way around the rock before he realized that he was now alone at Lick Creek swimming hole. The water flowed silently past the rocks and the beaten-down grass along the bank. A bird whispered in some near-by tree, and there was the genuine air of solitude about the hole that guaranteed abandonment.

The first fine burst of relieved feelings inside him gave way to disappointment which was succeeded by chagrin which was succeeded—now that Red Spingarn had gone elsewhere—by a profound anger against Red Spingarn.

Martin climbed miserably out upon the bank to dress. He shook himself, and after pausing a moment to dry in the sun, he made his way up the bank.

It was then that Martin learned the penalty of his assault on Red Spingarn.

His clothes, which had been in a neat little pile, were nowhere in sight.

Martin was as naked as a Mexican hairless puppy.

He was a mile from town on a bright summer day when the ceiling and visibility were unlimited.

Martin looked up the creek toward the town. Then he turned to regard the woodland behind him. He did not have to make the decision himself; it was forced upon him. He took to the woods.

Martin Butterfield was less equipped for the wilderness than even Sitting Bull. For Martin lacked not only a rifle and a handful of salt; he also was minus a breechclout.

The story of Martin's homeward trip that afternoon and evening is the chronicle of a march overland, the marcher keeping to cover and carefully avoiding all inhabited areas. Because there was no woodland within a quarter of a mile of his father's place, the end of the march was postponed perforce until darkness. Martin did not arrive home until after eight o'clock.

His arrival was not achieved on a triumphant note; rather, it was probably the most surreptitious reaching of a destination since a general named Hannibal sneaked a train of elephants over the Alps.

In short, Martin slipped up the front stairs, hoping that nobody in the brightly lighted kitchen and dining room to the rear would notice his arrival.

Having already guaranteed himself certain hardships by failure to mow the lawn and further hardships resulting from lateness, he had no desire to present himself nude and scratched and bruised. Somehow, this seemed to him now the worst of his offenses.

Upstairs he quietly donned clean clothing—without washing, of course, because the running water would have attracted attention.

After combing his hair he braced himself at the top of the steps. How best to meet such a delicate problem? He decided on the casual nothing-whatever-has-happened approach.

Martin Butterfield marched loudly down the stairs and into the kitchen, prepared to pass the time of day with his parents and thus ameliorate as far as possible any rancor that might be awaiting him.

For the second time that day, he had prepared himself for a crisis that failed to materialize.

The kitchen was empty.

Martin surveyed the brightly lighted room. The table was set and dinner was on the stove. Lamb chops and peas and mashed potatoes, the last-named now somewhat dry.

Martin was not fazed by the coldness of the food. Pondering the curious behavior of grown-ups, he heated up the food briskly, so briskly that smoke began to rise from the skillet of chops and a wisp or two of haze lingered over the potatoes.

But Martin was hungry and hunger made him impatient. He turned off the gas beneath the pots and kettles and loaded a plate. Sitting up to the table, he was enjoying the fortification of the inner man when the phone rang.

It was Mr. Buckmaster, the grocer.

"Oh, Martin?" he said. "Is your dad there or is he down at the creek?"

"He's not here . . ." Martin began.

"Well, then I'll go down to the swimming hole," Mr. Buckmaster said. "I just got back in town and heard about some kid drowning down there. You tell him I'm on my way if he comes back there."

"Somebody drownded?" Martin asked. But Mr. Buckmaster had hung up.

Martin put the receiver back in its cradle. No wonder his folks were gone! A drowning, and he had missed it!

He passed through the front door into the darkness, without another pang of hunger.

He wondered who it was. For a moment he suffered the terrible thought that maybe Red Spingarn had drowned after he, Martin Butterfield, had kicked him. Then he remembered that he had clearly heard Red's voice after that incident. However, he thought tentatively, if somebody *had* to get drowned, who deserved it more than . . . he cut off that thought. Bad luck to think such thoughts.

The time it took Martin to traverse the distance to the swimming hole in the darkness was in remarkable contrast to that consumed by his recent trip back from that point.

From half a mile away he could see the great floodlights and he could hear the voices. In the darkness, going down the road, he passed many slower pedestrians, but he had no time to pause for parleying.

Probably Sparky Roberts had been there the whole time, and had seen everything and now Martin would have to sit and hear it all secondhand. . . .

From a distance Martin could see the volunteer fire company's boat out in the creek, and he thought he could make out his father's form in the bow. When Martin grew up, he resolved, he would not waste an instant in getting into the fire company. Every day, something new and interesting.

As he came up to the edge of the crowd, he shaded his eyes in the glare of the light and looked about him.

There was plenty of movement down along the water's edge as volunteer firemen worked and men and women moved back and forth.

It took Martin quite a while to locate Sparky Roberts. At the moment he found him, Sparky, who was standing with his mother, turned and recognized Martin.

Martin instantly adopted the bland attitude of having been there all the time—before Sparky even knew anything about it.

"Do they know who it is yet?" Martin asked.

Sparky only looked blank and then, truly speechless, he tugged Mrs. Roberts' skirt and pointed.

Mrs. Roberts was much more articulate. She let out a shriek, as if she had seen a ghost.

The crowd turned and, for the second time in two days, Martin Butterfield found himself the utter, complete center of attraction.

In the silence, Sparky Roberts' voice was clear and lucid on the evening air:

"Martin didn't get drownded after all, did you, Martin?"

It was simply a friendly inquiry but it suddenly caused some bits and pieces of a puzzle to fall together in Martin's mind.

They had thought *he* was the one who got drownded!

How wonderful!

It was like yesterday on the bridge for a moment—only better.

For no reason at all, Mrs. Butterfield came hastily through the crowd and made an affectionate grab for him. But Martin eluded her as well as he could. This was no place for baby stuff.

"Thank heavens, thank heavens, thank heavens . . ." Mrs. Butterfield couldn't seem to think of another single thing to say.

Even his father, who certainly must be mad about that unmowed lawn, gave out a whoop.

There was a lovely uproar—initially.

"What happened, Martin? Where were you? We've been going crazy ever since we talked to Red Spingarn and he . . ."

Martin thought deeply while his father went on. He had to be careful of his words before so many people.

"I was a little late for supper," he said finally, committing himself to nothing whatever.

He looked up at his mother's face, shining not only with tears but with a certain beauty.

Then he looked up at his father. But his father was blowing his nose, and his handkerchief concealed everything but his dark, questioning eyes and his big black brows.

Somehow Martin had an uncomfortable suspicion that Mr. Butterfield would presently recover sufficiently to ask a few questions about how Martin happened to be swimming when he was supposed to be mowing.

It was a good time to change the subject.

"It sure is a big crowd," Martin said.

From the rear of the assemblage, Mr. Buckmaster, the grocer, could be heard clearly saying,

"A few more crowds like this and I resign as chief of the fire department."

All the way home, sitting on the front seat of the Butterfield car between his father and mother, Martin wondered what Mr. Buckmaster had meant. Instinctively, he felt it a wise policy not to ask. There was going to be enough trouble, he figured, over that unmowed lawn.

In any danger-fraught situation, it is usually advisable to adjust one's actions to suit the danger. The good sailor tacks to meet a shift in the wind; the baseball pitcher throws a change-of-pace ball. Martin Butterfield abruptly shifted his parents' thoughts to a new course.

"I ain't mad at Red Spingarn for drownding me," he said meekly. "I hope he gives my clothes back, though, 'cause I'd sure hate to lose the clothes that Dad worked so hard to get me . . ."

Thus Martin threw a little spotlight on his own, creditable generous nature, possibly obscuring his dubious record for the day.

And it worked—at least, in the case of Mrs. Butterfield. She looked down upon him with the absolute contentment of a mother who sees in her child a perfectly innocent heart.

Mr. Butterfield also looked down upon Martin.

"Very good of you to say so," he remarked. He might have said more except that his wife's hand on his shoulder warned him against any irritable parental conduct.

So he looked straight ahead as he drove into the Butterfield driveway.

Confound it, a heroic son *was* more than he could bear.

CHAPTER 3

In Which the Lawn Gets Cut

The relationship between parent and offspring is
seldom what speakers at father-and-son banquets
say it is. Quite otherwise.

Mr. Butterfield reflected on this sobering idea
for some little time after he put the ebony telephone back
in its cradle on his desk. It was only about nine in the morning, and Mr. Butterfield had a busy day ahead of him, his first
appointment only half an hour away; after that, the steady,
unabating stream of people who comprise a busy lawyer's
day.

He stood up and walked to the window of his office and
leaned against the frame, looking down in the street of the
village where the sun lay brightly on the store fronts and on
the heads of citizens of Fern Township early about their
shopping and business chores.

Mr. Butterfield gazed down without seeing, and he pondered the words of his wife over the telephone just now.

Ordinarily he did not pay much attention to those child
psychology books his wife read. Martha knew many rules
and laws about child-raising that he, Mr. Butterfield, didn't

know; he could not remember that such rules and laws were in effect when he was a boy. It made him feel momentarily as old as he imagined his son, Martin, aged ten, thought his father was.

But maybe Martha was right this time. Perhaps, having been so busy getting his law practice firmly established in these last few years, he had not given a proper share of his time, interest, and talent to his son.

If Martin seemed unable to escape spectacular entanglements, maybe it was Mr. Butterfield's fault as a parent, just as Martha said.

Mr. Butterfield drew his astonishingly big black brows together and looked out the window. He felt a sudden compassion and pity for little Martin, his son, and he made a resolve that he meant to carry out as soon as possible. Sighing, he thought of the heavy schedule of appointments that lay ahead of him that day—a couple of them were concerned with the Griffith lawsuit. Old man Griffith was important. His case was important too; victory in it would unquestionably add luster to the gold letters on the Butterfield office door. Yet those very appointments prevented him from acting immediately . . .

He thought slowly. There was *always* something that prevented him from acting . . . just as Martha had said.

"You've got to think of Martin ahead of business," she had admonished him.

In that moment, Mr. Butterfield made an important decision about the future of his son, Martin Butterfield.

He would not delay.

Turning from the window, he walked over and pressed the buzzer on his desk.

The door opened in a moment and his secretary stepped in, armed with her pad for dictation.

32

"Miss Marble," Mr. Butterfield said heavily, "please cancel all my appointments for today."

Miss Marble was somewhat older than her employer, and she had worked for attorneys long enough to be a young lawyer's mentor and advisor.

"What about the Griffith case, Mr. Butterfield?" she asked quietly. "That's—"

"No," said Mr. Butterfield with a certain deep, noble singleness of purpose not to be deflected, "something far more important has come up . . ."

The object of these troubled parental considerations was in the back yard of his parents' home at the precise moment his mother and father finished their conversation on the telephone. He was sitting on the step of the old barn entrance at the rear of the lot contemplating a very small, very bright-eyed garter snake that he had just captured near the dog kennels.

He did not know that he was ill-adjusted to his environment nor that he was developing behavior patterns that boded ill for the future. In fact, if he had been asked at that particular moment about his prospects in the years to come, he would have had a ready answer:

"I think I'll be a snake charmer and be in a show, like the man at the fire department's carnival last year."

He sat there quietly in the sun and studied the little gray snake whose neck he held delicately between thumb and forefinger.

Martin approached his victim with that detached, objective spirit that bespeaks the inquiring, scientific mind—the kind of intellect whose lively curiosity solved the law of gravity and discovered the great force of electricity.

Martin discovered, for example, that by squeezing his

33

thumb and forefinger together, the little snake could be made to dart its tongue at a great rate.

This discovery caused certain immediate hardships for the snake, whose little tail was curled miserably around Martin's wrist.

Martin sat there dreamily and foresaw the day when he would descend into a canvas pit inside a carnival tent. There would be a mass of heads peering over the side of the pit— Mr. Buckmaster, Red Spingarn, Sparky Roberts and there at the farthest corner, almost afraid to look but also afraid she might miss something heroic, Georgianna Semple, the brightest and most beautiful girl in the fifth-grade-to-be of the next September.

... Martin Butterfield, wearing white breeches and black knee boots, dropped cautiously, but with sufficient care-lessness to indicate his complete command of the situation, into the canvas pit where curled the pythons and the boa constrictors. There was nothing small, not even a rattle-snake, in the show of Martin Butterfield, the World's Cham-pion Snake Charmer. . . . Martin approached the largest python and, with one darting thrust, captured it by the neck. . . .

The little garter snake coiled on Martin's wrist suffered then in a cause about which it could not possibly know anything.

Martin was instantly sorry for squeezing its neck so hard. It might expire there in the morning sun before he could flaunt it in the face of Sparky Roberts. Sparky Roberts did not own any snakes, or at least, he didn't own any right now.

Martin let the snake get its wind in the palm of his hand, but it did not recuperate very rapidly. It just lay there wearily.

Life is too swift a thing, at the age of ten, to waste much time waiting. So Martin stood up, stretched, yawned, and took his captive inside the barn, where he placed it in the cool depths of Mrs. Butterfield's laundry hamper near the stationary tubs and electric washer. He did not remove the bed sheets that lay in the bottom of the hamper because they made a comfortable place for a convalescing snake. U. S. 728736

The day was still new and Martin still had time to consider its possibilities. His father had not said anything about lawn mowing this morning. Although the lawn had not been mowed yesterday, Martin felt no sense of compulsion to mow it today. One day is separate from another and if his father had wanted the grass cut today, he would have said so. Martin could not help it if his father was always changing his mind about what he wanted done.

Martin investigated his father's workbench against one wall of an old horsestall. The tools were all locked up in a large case beneath the heavy planking where hung Mr. Butterfield's big vise.

Martin felt the sudden urge to build something, to make something, to create, to add to the world. But he had no tools and there was no way of getting any right now, barring the use of a hacksaw (which latter was foresightedly locked up in Mr. Butterfield's chest).

Then occurred in Martin a sudden, deep, surging longing for the unobtainable. He really *needed* a set of tools—of his very own. Some of those small tools, such as any five-and-ten-cent store sells.

The chain of reasoning that followed would have been very interesting to Mr. Butterfield. When the chain was complete, Martin was busily mowing grass beside the house.

He moved the lawn mower up and down the deep, thick green carpet, making narrow, clean, thorough corridors with the whirling steel blades. Martin Butterfield, wanting a set of new tools for the new machine shop and building contractor's workbench that he was going to set up, mowed the grass in exactly the manner his father always recommended. Martin left none of the usual telltale lines of grass standing between lawn-mower swipes.

He was all conscience this morning. He humbly regretted his failure to follow his father's advice the day before. He felt an overpowering sense of shame at having worried his parents so much last night. He suddenly revered and admired his elders with a humility that would have done Mrs. Butterfield more good than three issues of her favorite child psychology magazine.

Martin really wanted that tool set.

When Sparky Roberts, the friend of his bosom, shouted over the back fence, Martin kept the lawn mower moving and pretended not to hear. "Hey, Martin!"

Martin was not to be deterred from his honest effort at work and reform by the first temptation that drifted past him on the summer breeze.

In a moment, Sparky was walking up and down beside the mower of the grass asking questions that could neither be heard nor be answered in the clashing metallic din of lawn-mower blades. Martin did not stop work until Sparky gave every sign of making ready to abandon his pursuit. Then and only then did he halt, to rest impressively and to deal haughtily with persons who had nothing better to do than annoy and harry a busy, energetic, working boy.

"For goodness sake, Sparky," he said, "can't you see I'm busy?"

Although this fact must have been obvious to people living two blocks down the street, it did not seem an improper observation to either of the boys.

"Your father must be awful mad or else you wouldn't be working so hard, Martin," said Sparky curiously. "Did he lick you good for last night?"

There was just a faint trace of delicious, eager hope in the question.

Martin looked pained.

"Can't a man work if he *wants* to?" Martin inquired.

If Martin's earlier efforts to astonish Sparky had failed, this gambit more than made up for previous deficits.

Sparky sat down in the grass and looked around.

"You ain't kiddin' me, Martin," he said. "You got something up your sleeve and you ain't tellin' it."

The accuracy of this analysis was sufficient to cause Martin to redouble his look of pain and then redouble that. Meanwhile he had a counterstroke to deliver.

"You know so much, Sparky Roberts," he replied, "that maybe you know what I got in the barn that I ain't going to show you—just for that."

"You ain't got nothin'," Sparky replied. "Every time you get in a pinch, you always got something new to give somebody or show somebody or trade somebody; and it's never nothing except what you make up in your head."

Martin adopted the resigned look of a person robbed of the opportunity of doing someone else a favor.

"Okay," he said quietly. Grasping the lawn-mower handles, he set up a din that exceeded every known sound effect in the field of grass cutting.

He was not surprised when Sparky fell into step with him as he moved over the grass.

"What have you got?" Sparky yelled.

"Nothin'," shouted Martin. "You said I didn't have anything, didn't you?"

Martin toyed with Sparky for three trips up and down the lawn before he revealed the existence of the serpent. Then he exacted three round trips of grass cutting from Sparky while he went to the barn himself and got the snake.

It was still in a somnolent state and Sparky Roberts was

not only chagrined at its lack of serpentine fury but also by its lack of size, a characteristic not emphasized by Martin in his preliminary description.

"You cheated," Sparky said. "That snake ain't even worth one cut with your old lawn mower."

"You can just get out of my yard then," Martin advised.

"And you can stay out of mine," Sparky returned. "If I ever catch you in my yard, I'll—"

"You're in mine now," Martin said more quietly, reminding himself of Sparky's physical prowess, "and you better watch out—"

He looked at his snake and, before continuing his conversation with his friend, it appeared necessary to Martin to put the small reptile back in the laundry hamper out of the sun and heat for further recovery.

He returned from the barn in time to see Sparky leaping over the front hedge.

The friends exchanged parting salutes.

"You remember what I told you," Sparky called from the neutral combat ground of the street.

"You stay out of my yard," Martin replied, returning to the lawn mower and to the industrious performance of his self-imposed duties.

He marched off behind his spinning machine, plowing up a small green tornado as he proceeded to work with the formidable humility of spirit of the man who knows he is demonstrating a great capacity for good among a world of lesser fellows.

It was thus, in fact, that Mr. Butterfield, walking up the shady street from the village, found his son. At first the attorney could not credit his ears with the error of hearing the sound of work in the Butterfield yard; however, when he arrived at the hedge and looked over into his own grassy plot, his ears proved to have been correct.

Mr. Butterfield thought that Martin had not seen him arrive and, in truth, Martin gave an excellent facsimile of that very aspect, although he was rather surprised to note the arrival of his father in mid-morning.

"What are you doing, Martin?" Mr. Butterfield asked with a vagueness that could be excused on the grounds of surprise.

"Just mowing the grass, Dad," Martin replied. In his present self-righteous frame of mind Martin could not remember when he had not *liked* mowing grass.

Martin did not have time now, particularly now, even to talk to his father. If ever a circumstance were tailor-made for leaving a good imprint upon his father, Martin figured, this was it. He trundled the lawn mower right past his waiting parent with such devotion to the job that he could not spare the effort for passing the time of day.

Mr. Butterfield stood on the walk that wound around his home and felt not a little deflated. He deserved a better fate than this.

Deflation was just at the point of giving way to irritation when Mrs. Butterfield stepped into the yard and found her husband.

"George!" she said. "What are you doing here? Did you forget something?"

That did it.

"You'd think I was just so much excess baggage around here," he mumbled.

His wife was at his side.

"Anything wrong, George?" she inquired, looking up at him with intent eyes.

"Good grief!" Mr. Butterfield snorted. "Can't a man just come home to be with his family—"

"Do you have a headache?" Mrs. Butterfield asked. "I'll get you some aspirin or something—"

The lawn mower passed stoutly and loudly, drowning the remainder of Mrs. Butterfield's prescription.

When Martin was adequately distant, Mr. Butterfield took his wife gently but firmly by the elbow.

"I came home," he said righteously, "to spend a day with Martin, as you suggested."

Mrs. Butterfield looked properly surprised at such prompt action on any suggestion of hers.

"I'm going into the house and change my clothes," Mr. Butterfield added. "Maybe Martin would like to go trout fishing—for a change."

"I'm sure he would," said Mrs. Butterfield, with the resolute sympathy born of having one of her ideas implemented by her husband.

The Butterfield parents retired to the house, and Mr. Butterfield, leaving his wife in the kitchen, went upstairs and changed to an old suit of khakis left over from his days in the air force in the late war.

While he donned, with slowly growing contentment, these clothes that always signified a day of outdoor sport, he wondered why he had never before been tempted to taste of the pleasure of doing something irregular, of breaking his routine, and enjoying life with his boy, who would only be a boy once.

The sound of the lawn mower, the serenity of the summer morning, and the prospect of a day with no commitments of any kind combined to give Mr. Butterfield a blessed boyish feeling. Such was the coltish mood that was upon him when he rejoined his busy son in the yard.

The project of grass cutting was going noisily forward with the kind of resolution that usually springs from the intention of receiving an immediate, concrete reward, in this case one set of tools with which to build a wonderful something, as yet undecided.

It took Mr. Butterfield only a moment to observe that the grass-cutting job was nearly finished. It was an opportune time for him to have taken an interest in Martin, he felt.

"Swell, Martin," he said in a very man-to-man fashion. "You'll be finished in a couple of minutes now, and then maybe we can go fishing."

Now a day of fishing was ordinarily regarded by Martin Butterfield as a day well spent, but hardly as a reward for such valuable service as he was just now rendering.

He stopped behind the lawn mower and glanced at his father.

"Don't you have to work today, Dad?" he inquired in a tone of voice that he had frequently heard asking *him*, "Don't you have any homework to do tonight, Martin?"

"Uh—well, no," his father replied, understandably disconcerted. "I guess I don't have to work if I don't want to."

Martin reflected on the announcement of so wayward a philosophy.

Martin reflected on something else too. He had obviously made a tactical mistake by mowing the lawn so swiftly; it was true that he was now nearly finished.

"I don't think I can go fishing," he said. "I got too much to do."

Mr. Butterfield said, "What?"

"I think I'll clean out the cellar and straighten up the workbench in the barn," Martin said, adding the latter task as a good entering wedge on the subject of tools.

Mr. Butterfield stroked his chin and then, without saying anything further, went into the house via the back door, leaving Martin to finish the mowing.

The day was not working out quite as Mr. Butterfield had imagined it would.

In the pantry, he paused over the cookie jar, absently extracting a chocolate chip cookie and munching it thoughtfully while his wife filled a laundry bag with clothing in the kitchen.

"I thought you were going fishing," Mrs. Butterfield said.

Mr. Butterfield gazed thoughtfully at his wife. "Did you tell Martin to clean the cellar and straighten up the workbench in the barn?" he inquired.

"No," said Mrs. Butterfield. "Why?"

"Nothing," replied her husband.

Awe and curiosity in Mr. Butterfield were now replaced by slow irritation.

He finished the cookie and, without speaking again, went out to the barn at the rear of the lot where, among other equipment, rested his fishing tackle.

Confound it, he fumed slowly, Martin Butterfield was going trout fishing whether he liked it or not. He, Attorney Butterfield, had not canceled a lot of important appointments for nothing.

No more nonsense now.

He selected a rod and filled a creel with bits of tackle, jars of salmon eggs and some felt pads of dry flies. Properly loaded up, he went back out into the sunshine, meeting his wife taking her laundry to the barn for the weekly washing there.

The noise of the lawn mower in the yard had ceased now and Martin was nowhere visible. However, he was audible. There were mighty sounds of movement and of house cleaning in the vegetable cellar at the rear of the house.

In order to insure the fact that his work was not unnoticed, Martin took means to call it to his parents' attention. From the darkness of the cellar, his voice came.

"I'll just sprout these potatoes before they all go to waste," he said.

Mr. Butterfield's eyes met his wife's. She was obviously gratified by this announcement; she appeared to feel that all

her confidence in Martin was vindicated and that Mr. Butterfield should be ashamed of himself for his doubts.

"He certainly is energetic," she said. "There's one thing
about Martin, when he starts something, he—"

Mr. Butterfield interrupted. "Do you suppose he's sick?"

Mrs. Butterfield reproved him with a glance. Tossing her
head, she went on to the barn.

Martin emerged from the dirt cellar briefly and with adequate grime to evidence his labors.

"That place is a mess," he said to nobody in particular but
with an accusing note that Mr. Butterfield accepted personally.

"Did you just notice that?" his father inquired.

Martin looked at the tackle. "Well, Dad," he said, "I hope
you catch something."

If his father would only go away and leave him alone with
his mother, Martin thought, he might have that set of tools—
or the money to buy it—no later than noon. If only his father
would get out of the way. . . .

"How much do you think all this work is worth, Martin?"
his father asked.

It was the sudden piercing question of a lawyer who has
treated a witness with kindness and patience for too long.

"Worth?" Martin repeated questioningly, as if the word
presented an utterly new viewpoint on his noble efforts. "I
thought—well, there's a lot of things ought to be done around
here, Dad. I'd like to fix everything up this summer. Course
I haven't got the tools to do what I *could* do."

Mr. Butterfield turned and looked at the jury triumphantly, but the jury was out in the barn where she could
not hear this revealing reply.

Mr. Butterfield felt fine. "Okay, Martin," he said, "I'll get
you some tools. Only you have to go fishing with me today."

A man ought to get some reward for listening to the

experts on child psychology, and Mr. Butterfield considered a day's trout fishing to be an excellent dividend for the trouble and disappointment he had encountered so far this morning.

The speed with which the cellar cleaning was abandoned was a surprise to nobody but Mrs. Butterfield, who only saw her son streak into the barn long enough to snatch down his rod and reel.

"You going, too?" she asked, looking up.

"Dad wants me to," Martin said dutifully, disappearing out the door into the sunshine.

The two men of the Butterfield family climbed into the family car in front of the house just a moment too late.

Mrs. Butterfield emptied the bag of laundry from the house into one of the stationary tubs and turned the water on. Then she opened the hamper that had been standing in the barn all week.

When she reached in to pluck out the bed sheets in the bottom, the cry which rose from her bosom could not have been more compelling if she had actually seized one of the boa constrictors in the imaginary pit of the World's Champion Snake Charmer, Martin Butterfield.

Mr. Butterfield arrived a good twenty strides ahead of his agile son, but a good thirty seconds after Mrs. Butterfield had clasped the first garter snake that had ever come personally into her life.

As described above, the males of the Butterfield household were just a moment too late in their departure.

Mrs. Butterfield's initial shock changed as rapidly as feminine emotions can change from fright to terror to weakness.

Martin Butterfield recognized none of these changes. He was too busy at the last fatal moment, noticing that his snake was rapidly escaping over the threshold of the barn door toward some shrubs near by.

"Mother!" he cried. "You're lettin' my snake get away!"

It was astonishing to observe the speed with which Mrs. Butterfield's emotions crystallized into a mood that Mr. Butterfield easily recognized.

"Martin!" she gasped. "Did you put that snake in the barn?"

She leaned weakly on her husband's shoulder. "It was right in the laundry," she said.

Mr. Butterfield patted her. "It was only a little one," he said rather illogically, as if size would help the situation.

While his mother was being thus consoled, Martin was quietly engaged in recapturing his victim. No use losing a good snake.

He was just turning toward the barn door to find a new place to keep his pet, where it wouldn't be bothered, when his mother stepped out into the sunshine and took him briskly by the ear. Snake and all, Martin found himself suddenly propelled toward the house.

Over his shoulder, he heard his father say, "But we were going fishing —"

"You go back to the office," said Mrs. Butterfield in a low, even, authoritative voice that warned all comers against argument.

Martin could not look around to witness his father's surprise because of certain circumstances related to his ear. He did not hear his father mumble some words about child psychology.

Martin marched steadily forward toward the privacy of the Butterfield kitchen and a study in child psychology that he understood with particular feeling in a certain area of his trousers.

CHAPTER 4

The Boy Bugler

MARTIN BUTTERFIELD differed from his parents in the two distinct ways that most boys differ from grown-ups. Not only did Martin know when he had had enough, but he also was constitutionally unable to waste much time in licking his wounds. There were enough affairs, ideas and natural wonders in this interesting world to entrance him and thus take his mind off his troubles, however long and involved those troubles may have appeared to such a casual outsider as his father.

Martin went to bed on the evening of his great and misdirected efforts at snake-raising without so much as a recollection that he had ever desired a snake for a pet, much less paid a pants-warming price in retribution for so harmless a desire.

Martin felt fine as he undressed for bed. Another day lay just beyond the night he was now to waste in sleep; just what it held for Martin Butterfield was not exactly known to Martin, but he was serenely confident that he would be equal to its opportunities.

When he laid his head upon the pillow, he automatically closed out one day with neither regret nor self-congratulation.

How different from adults! How remarkably different from the mother and father who sat in the living room downstairs reflecting upon the selfsame day that Martin had just forgotten! Mr. and Mrs. Butterfield were quietly casting up sums of conduct, and coming out with a dismal total after each exercise in addition.

Mrs. Butterfield, who had urged excellent child psychology upon her husband that very morning, might have been thought ready to abandon study of that science forever. Here is one example of the difference between grown-ups and children: having been burned once, the adult immediately returns to be burned again.

Mrs. Butterfield was unhappily leafing through her favorite child-guidance magazine.

Meanwhile her husband was trying to read the paper. Had he learned anything? Not visibly. At this very moment he was considering how best he could establish closer contact with his little son—get next to the boy and assist him in this trying period of his life.

The object of these affectionate concerns was already drifting off to a dreamless sleep upstairs, oblivious even of the fact that he was going through a troublesome time, but that made no difference to his parents. Parents, being adult, are not inclined to permit each day to take care of itself, as it adequately would.

Adults must remember yesterday and regret it, prepare for tomorrow and worry about it.

There was a leaden silence in the living room, broken only by the rustle of Mrs. Butterfield's magazine and Mr. Butterfield's edition of the evening paper.

Mrs. Butterfield broke the silence. Her tone had lost some

of the sureness and confidence that characterized certain advice she had given her husband earlier that day.

"Do you think other people have as much trouble with their children as we have with Martin, George?" she asked.

Mr. Butterfield looked over his paper, as if "trouble" were a word he didn't understand.

"We don't have any real trouble," he sparred.

"Don't dodge the issue, George," she replied. "That's just like you. You'd say that if the roof fell in."

Mr. Butterfield, cornered by the clarity of this feminine point of view, protected himself by making a suggestion that would never have occurred to him if he had not felt compelled to come up with some idea—any idea.

"Maybe," he said, "it might help if we sent Martin to some nice boys' camp . . ."

It was only a vague, wild something to talk about. He really hadn't meant it.

By such slender chances are great events put into motion.

"You know," Mrs. Butterfield replied, her tired, pretty face livening, "that's the very thing I've had in the back of my head all evening—some camp where Martin could learn responsibility and obedience to authority and coöperation."

Without looking in the magazine Mrs. Butterfield held in her hand, Mr. Butterfield recognized the language. He had got himself out of a corner all right, and into something he hadn't planned.

Before he could speak, his wife was already outlining an idea that seemed to have been waiting to spring full-grown upon the scene.

"There's a wonderful camp," she said, "where the Larrabees always send little Lawrence."

Mr. Butterfield plaited his large, black eyebrows. "Isn't little Lawrence, as you call him, one of Martin's dearest enemies?" he inquired. "Isn't he the boy Martin refers to as That Stinker?"

Mrs. Butterfield bridled. "That was a long time ago," she said primly.

"I don't notice that Martin plays with him much," Mr. Butterfield observed.

"He's away at school most of the time, as you very well know," Mrs. Butterfield replied.

"Oh," said Mr. Butterfield. He hoped that Martin would enjoy whatever camp it was that he, Mr. Butterfield, could not now very well prevent him from attending.

Major Lake's mountain camp for boys was a study in measured roughing-it, a log mess hall in the middle of a greensward parade with four groups of platformed tents spaced at some hundreds of yards distance on the fringe of the forest.

It was an establishment whose quiet, dignified advertisements in excellent magazines proclaimed it modestly as a place that developed "the inner man, without neglecting the outer boy."

Major Lake was an old army man, a cavalry officer unhorsed. He was a wiry brown little figure, tanned to a fantastic coffee color by a fantastic devotion to the outdoors. His little silver mustache was a glistening bit of ermine against his brown skin which was adequately exhibited below his tropical shorts and short sleeves and at the throat of his V-necked shirt.

Major Lake stood erectly before his desk that morning in June waiting for the three boys who were now coming through the adjoining mess hall to his office.

He always was waiting and ready when boys arrived. It was an example of preparedness as well as courtesy, not to mention punctuality.

When the three boys entered, following the college-boy camp counselor, Major Lake came stiffly to attention. He bowed from the hips as the trio lined up instinctively in military fashion before him. Then he shook hands gravely all around.

"Hello, Larrabee," he said gruffly, taking the hand of a neatly dressed boy with neatly brushed blond curls and a pair of eyes as alert and bright as those of a lively mouse.

"How do you do, Major," replied Lawrence Larrabee, known in some quarters as That Stinker.

Lawrence turned to his two comrades.

"This is Martin Butterfield," he said, pointing to a boy obviously less neat than himself, "and this is Sparky Roberts."

Martin Butterfield and Sparky Roberts mumbled and shook hands, instantly regretting having delivered their travel-stained little paws so confidingly into the iron grip of the major.

It had been a long and tedious trip for both of them. They had been, and were now, at a disadvantage in the presence of Lawrence Larrabee, who was at no pains to conceal his superiority over a couple of chumps who had never before been to summer camp.

In fact, the plunge into a summer camp was so sudden for Martin and Sparky that both were a little taxed to realize that the adventure was already upon them. Martin's parents had sprung the idea without any more reason than grown-ups usually need; by a process known as keeping-up-with-the-Joneses, Sparky Roberts found himself sharing Martin's good fortune.

It was lucky that Sparky could come. Martin could not have borne Lawrence Larrabee alone. In fact, he had hardly been able to bear his half of Lawrence all the way up from

Fern Township on the train. Lawrence had known all about talking to railroad conductors, porters, and brakemen. He had also known all about eating in a dining car. It was entirely possible that two weeks of camping with Lawrence Larrabee might develop Martin's character in a way his mother had not anticipated.

Martin tried to pay attention to Major Lake as the camp director delivered his welcoming speech. But he was in no condition to concentrate on anything except certain pleasurable thoughts pertaining to bodily assault upon Stinky Larrabee.

". . . and now," the major was saying as Martin brought his limited attentive powers to bear, "I'll see that you three chaps get quarters in the same section—the North Outpost. You know the North Outpost, Larrabee, old boy?"

"Yes, sir," replied Lawrence Larrabee. "I'll show the new boys the ropes, sir."

"Righto," said the major cheerily, clicking his heels together.

The major almost saluted. Lawrence Larrabee clicked his heels in an admirably practiced imitation before turning and following the counselor toward the veranda of the mess hall, where the three campers had left their duffel bags, which had now disappeared.

"Hey, somebody stole our stuff," Sparky Roberts said indignantly.

Martin was wholly prepared to accept this theory when Lawrence Larrabee imparted some information.

"You dopes," he said, "the camp truck took the stuff up to the North Outpost. How long is it going to take you greenhorns to catch on, anyway?"

The greenhorns bore their humiliation in silence, being in strange and hostile country. They followed Lawrence and the counselor across the green parade toward the group of tan tents that comprised the North Outpost of Major Lake's establishment.

At the North Outpost they found that they were to be quartered cosily in the same tent where they could better develop their coöperative spirits.

The counselor, who was a healthy young collegian with a dark, close-clipped crop of hair and a casual briskness, made them feel at home before departing.

"Put your gear under the cots, and make it neat!" he ordered. "Then wash and get ready for supper. No fooling around!"

The counselor glared at his charges in a manner not forecast in Major Lake's camp advertisements.

Martin and Sparky sat down on their cots and watched Lawrence Larrabee busily put the counselor's words into effect as far as his personal affairs were concerned.

"How long is two weeks?" Martin asked Sparky Roberts.

Sparky thought. "Seems like forever," he said dismally.

Lawrence Larrabee, who spent his winters away at school, regarded both of them with an air of speculation as he unpacked his duffel bags.

"You better get your stuff done," he said, "or that counselor will stick you in the kitchen doing K.P."

"What's—" Martin checked himself but not before his curiosity had revealed his ignorance once more.

"Don't know what K.P. is?" taunted Lawrence. "Don't know anything, do you?"

Sparky Roberts roused himself. "I know what it is," he said. "You don't know so much."

The blond Master Larrabee looked up from the canvas bag in which he was probing.

"What is it, then?" he asked blithely, plunging again into the bag.

"Why should I tell you, if you don't know?" retorted Sparky.

"I do know what it is —"

"What did ya ask for then?"

"I didn't ask."

"You did too. Didn't he, Marty?"

"Sure, he did. He said —"

Martin paused, his eyes fastened on an object that Lawrence Larrabee had withdrawn from the depths of his duffel bag. At this moment, Martin lost all interest in the argument, in favor of a shining gold bugle held by Lawrence Larrabee.

"Wow!" Martin exclaimed. "Is that bugle yours?"

"Who else's?" answered Lawrence Larrabee in his kindest mood.

While two pairs of eyes watched enviously, That Stinker Larrabee lifted his shining instrument to his lips and tootled a couple of tentative, short notes.

"I'm the bugler of this camp," he announced. "I get to blow the bugle every morning and every noon and every night."

It was the heaviest blow of the day to Martin Butterfield, whose spirit of coöperation, obedience to authority and general character were now to undergo two weeks of intense development at Major Lake's camp for boys.

Living with the camp bugler, Martin Butterfield and Sparky Roberts were triply certain of awaking on time every morning. They first greeted the dawn when Lawrence Larrabee's alarm clock sounded for the little trumpeter to be up and doing. Then their sleep was further damaged when the bugler sounded a few soft test notes before venturing into the world outside. Finally, they were brought to their feet by the camp-wide, brassy cock's crow of

Lawrence Larrabee as he performed his highly public duties near the flagpole.

It might be thought that this unhappy situation would harden the heart of Martin Butterfield against all bugles for the remainder of his life. Such a conclusion does not take into consideration the peculiar obsessions that develop in the breast of man, ten or seventy winters old. Lawrence Larrabee's bugle, denied to Martin, became the passion of Martin's life, and bugling aspirations replaced any previous desire he may have had to live the dull life of G-man or Foreign Legionnaire.

After breakfast on the first morning in camp, Martin and Sparky sat on their cots and waited for assembly (more bugling).

"Do you think Lawrence might let us play his bugle a little?" Martin inquired of his friend.

"That Stinker!" replied Sparky. "Why don't you ask him?"

The opportunity presented itself instantly. Lawrence Larrabee, fresh from breakfast, climbed the steps to the wooden platform and entered the tent with his bugle under his arm.

"You two better make up your bunks for inspection," he said crisply, and he immediately fell to at his bunk, replacing his instrument in his duffel bag.

Martin and Sparky rose and made a gesture or two at their unmade beds.

"Could I borrow your bugle a minute, Lawrence?" Martin asked cautiously.

"Are you crazy?" replied Lawrence. "That bugle cost twenty-five dollars, and anyway I don't want you blowing germs all over it."

"*You* haven't got any germs, I guess," Sparky Roberts interjected unfortunately. "I guess you haven't —"

54

"Nobody's going to blow my bugle," Lawrence said conclusively, "except me."

Martin made his bed as well as he could, which was sufficient to get him two demerits when Major Lake inspected the camp that morning. It was consoling to learn that Sparky had been similarly rewarded. Meanwhile, Lawrence Larrabee escaped unmarked.

Martin spent the morning fruitlessly trying to prove that fire could be made by rubbing two sticks together. The counselor in woodsmanship, holding class on the shady bank of the brook flowing past the camp, demonstrated this remarkable fact early in the session, but something in the natural laws of friction seemed to have been repealed by the time Martin's turn came.

Furthermore, Martin and Sparky were much more interested in the discovery that Lawrence Larrabee was ticklish. Lawrence's ticklishness cost him two demerits before he "told" on Martin and Sparky, who were rewarded with an equal number, a price that was cheap, considering that the black marks against the name of Lawrence were not expunged thereby.

A wrestling match between Martin and Sparky shortly before lunch hour resulted in another demerit; a trifle of tardiness in arriving at the mess hall miraculously produced still another; and a bread roll thrown accurately at Lawrence Larrabee's ear added so substantially to Martin's total character-building activity for the morning that he not very surprisingly found himself on K.P. duty at 1.00 P.M., immediately after lunch.

K.P., he learned to his chagrin, had a good deal to do with washing and drying dishes and much more to do with Mr. Ed Slater, the camp cook and a former corporal in the United States Army, culinary department.

Mr. Slater was a tall, thin, bald, unmilitary figure in a

white skivvy shirt, white cap, and once-white trousers. He operated his galley on the theory that the army system was the correct system for instilling respect in young men and especially in juveniles who were privileged to eat his food.

"Get right in there up to your elbows, young fellow," he advised succinctly when Martin reported to the inferno of heat and steam, racked-up pots and kettles, dish pans and scalding tanks that constituted the realm where Mr. Slater cooked and lived and had his being.

Martin regarded the stack of metal trays and hillocks of cups and silverware that were suddenly his special province.

"Gee!" said Martin.

"Haw!" responded Mr. Slater. "If your mother had raised you right, you wouldn't be here."

Martin looked at the tall gentleman preparing to sit down at a dough board and eat his own lunch.

"Didn't you eat yet?" Martin inquired curiously.

"I never eat until all my little friends are fed," Mr. Slater said benignly. "It's the sunny side of my nature—also, the major don't allow me to."

Martin prepared for work, but not with sufficient speed to have passed muster in the old army.

"Now get goin', Martin," urged Mr. Slater. "If you work hard, I'll mebbe help you after I get a few vittles tucked away."

Martin plunged into the hot water. It was a memorable hour and a half. He broke only three cups, which Mr. Slater said was under par for the course.

During the ordeal Martin was amiable because it was clearly the healthful way.

"Do you live back here?" he asked, pointing to a door-way through which a bunk was clearly visible.

"I *exist* here," said Mr. Slater. "Nobody *lives* here except the major and he lives plenty okay."

Martin considered this fact and saw nothing remarkable in it. So he said nothing.

"A major always lives good," the cook said expansively. "He's a big shot, that's why. When you grow up, Martin, remember to be a big shot."

"I will," Martin said. And he *would* remember it, too, he thought.

Martin looked up to find the cook regarding him sternly.

"But don't be like the major, Martin," he said.

Martin dried a tray thoughtfully. He had not devoted much thought to the major up to the moment, having been thoroughly occupied with escaping the attention of that figure.

"No, sir," he replied with more tact than logic.

"You wanta know why, Martin?" the cook continued. "I'll tell you why. The major don't know little sour apples about running a camp."

Here Martin had a boy's disconcerting glimpse into the world of adulthood where everything is not always what it seems.

"He doesn't?" Martin inquired incredulously. "Then how does he run . . ."

"That's the way the world is, Martin," the cook replied affably. "Now you take a fellow like me—I was in the cavalry for nigh on to thirty years but I never lost my horse or even my cook wagon. But the major, he —"

Martin stopped work altogether. "Did the major lose his —"

The cook looked down upon Martin with the solemn and regretful mien of a policeman about to arrest his best friend.

"Yes, sir, Martin," the cook said, "me and the major was

57

in the army together and he sure did go and lose his horse one night. He even lost hisself and they had to send a party out to find him."

Martin could hardly wait to finish drying the dishes so that he could spread this alarming word.

But Ed Slater was forehanded.

"Mum's the word, Martin," he said. "Not a word of it to anybody. The major might not like it. . . . Now, let's get these dishes done."

All this was so interesting to Martin that he speeded up his efforts accordingly.

When Martin returned to his tent, he found Lawrence Larrabee lying restfully on his bunk, enjoying the closing moments of the camp rest period, while Sparky Roberts was illegally on his feet putting on his bathing trunks for swimming.

Lawrence greeted Martin affectionately.

"Major Lake says you're the worst behaved child in this camp."

"You watch out what you're saying," Martin warned darkly. "Don't call me a child. I'm a—a—a fellow."

Lawrence stared at the ceiling.

"The worst one in the camp, anyhow," Lawrence said.

Martin thought this over and accepted it as an implied apology for calling him a child.

The remainder of the rest period was spent pleasantly in stout argument on assorted subjects that made the time pass until swimming. After the swimming period, there were afternoon lessons in arts and crafts and then dinner.

Following dinner, Major Lake instructed the boys to remain in the mess hall for a period of letter writing, at which time Martin Butterfield developed symptoms of severe stomach-ache, influenza and more permanently damaging ailments which required his retirement to his tent, while less ingenious campers struggled painfully over a few words to their folks on the subject of the weather, camp life and please-send-me.

The ingenuity of Martin's maneuver did not dawn wholly upon him until he was lying stretched out on his cot reading the latest edition of *The Gorilla Kid*, an illustrated child's book not written by Hans Christian Andersen.

As he turned the comic book pages, he suddenly remembered the bugle—no, it would not be stealing—it would not be like stealing, either. He would only look. In a moment he was rummaging beneath Lawrence Larrabee's bunk, searching for the bugle. It was right there in the top of Lawrence's duffel bag.

Martin looked down into the bag at a constellation of glittering sparks from the shining golden curves of the instrument. It would not hurt to touch it.

In a moment he was fondling it and a second later he was trying the mouthpiece against his lips, hardly breathing. If only he had been fortunate enough to be alive during the Civil War, he could have blown the bugle that sent the cavalry charging—people had some sense then—if a boy wanted to go fight a war, he could go.

His reverie might have continued indefinitely, except for the sound of loud, school-is-out shouts from the direction of the mess hall. The letter writing was over.

Martin hastily tucked the bugle away in the duffel bag, leaped on his cot and began producing the reasonable facsimiles of sniffles, coughs and sneezes that had got him this brief period of freedom.

It was just as well that he went through this sound effect rehearsal, because his original plan to recover almost immediately was thwarted by an unforeseen occurrence.

Major Lake, in starched shorts and brisk manner, was ushered into the tent by Lawrence Larrabee.

59

"Here he is, Major," Lawrence said sweetly. "He looks pretty sick."

The major regarded Lawrence with open admiration of his sympathy for his little friend. Martin thereupon suffered such a genuine emotional disturbance at the conduct of Master Larrabee that he actually *did* look sick.

Major Lake looked down on Martin, mustaches bristling with agitation.

"We'll just keep you in bed for a day or two, old chap," he said, "and then we'll see if you don't feel better."

Martin would have shown signs of marked improvement if he had dared to. Instead, he mumbled something unintelligible.

"Better take off your clothes now and get under the covers, old chap," said Major Lake.

Martin sat up and began to undress while Major Lake and Lawrence Larrabee looked on.

"I guess he won't be able to go on the overnight hike tomorrow night, will he?" Lawrence Larrabee asked with tender concern for Martin's welfare.

"Hardly," said the major. "We'll have to fix him up a bit first."

"I think I—" Martin began, but thought better of it.

The major was sympathetically jolly, even with the worst child in the camp. "Cheer up, Butterfield," he said. "A good night's sleep will probably do the trick." He patted Martin on the shoulder.

"I'll see that he doesn't have to get up for his breakfast," Lawrence volunteered.

The major and Lawrence Larrabee passed out of the tent into the night, making way for Sparky Roberts, fresh from a bout with pen and ink.

Sparky was short and to the point.

"Martin," he said, "are you really sick or did you just do that to get out of that old letter you had to write?"

The patient exhibited symptoms of some hardihood.

"Wait till I get better," he said. "I'll fix that stinker Lawrence so he won't even be able to blow a bugle."

Not having been really ill at all, Martin Butterfield may not be said to have recovered from an illness. He could—and did—begin a rapid return to obvious health early in the first and only afternoon of his confinement, as early as he dared. His gain of strength was much accelerated for the simple reason that he had discovered the truth of an old adage of which he had never even heard, to wit: Ill blows the wind that profiteth nobody.

Being forced to remain abed contemplating his absence from the overnight hike, Martin Butterfield had conceived a very pearl of an idea.

Tonight everybody in camp except Martin and Ed Slater, the cook, would march out on a valley trail through the wilderness.

Mr. Slater would be asleep in his cook shack.

By simple addition of these two facts, Martin had arrived at a far more wonderful sum than he had ever found in the fourth-grade arithmetic class at Fern Township Public School; tonight he, Martin Butterfield, would be free to consider the bugle as an instrument and as a craftsman's tool. Nobody would hear him and nobody would ever know the difference, not even Lawrence Larrabee, who, Martin fervently hoped, might catch typhoid fever from Martin's own germs.

He could hardly wait for tonight's hike because he was not going.

After what seemed to be as long as a visit to the dentist, evening finally settled over the camp in the mountains. As darkness fell, dim figures moved about, shadows equipped with haversacks and belt knives and blanket rolls and flash lights and hip axes. Just as the full night, moonless and chilly, settled in the valley, Major Lake took his place at the head of his troops and marched out through the North Outpost, heading up a faint trail toward the mountains.

Martin felt a disturbing sense of sudden abandonment as he heard the scuffling footsteps and the bright clash of voices fade away up the woodland trail. But the clang of pots and kettles in the distant galley reminded him there was company in the camp; this knowledge warmed him, and he was further comforted by the imminence of an evening spent at bugling.

It was not hard for him to imagine how surprised his father and mother and friends would be when he finally raised his very own bugle—that he would acquire by unspecified means as soon as he got home—to play it like a Civil War bugle boy. Or at least, better than old Lawrence Larrabee ever played *his* bugle.

Martin arose from his bed and peered outside the tent. The night was black, but wisps of gray fog traced thin, wavy lines across its depths. The lights in the camp kitchen glowed as the old cook worked.

Martin breathed deeply. It was a fine evening, silent with that kind of silence that invites noisemaking in the same manner that an unbroken window in a haunted house invites a flying rock.

The hiking campers could no longer be heard when Martin went inside the tent and got the bugle. It was cold and slick in his hands and its yellow-gold sheen under the light reflected its precious nature.

For a long time Martin sat on the steps of his tent platform and breathed softly into the little horn, listening to its faint ringing note. It was only after he had sat there for a quarter of an hour that he noticed the galley lights had dimmed perceptibly. It was then that he realized a blanket of fog was settling over the camp, obscuring what little had been visible in the darkness.

Good. Even if he awakened Mr. Slater, the cook wouldn't be able to see where the noise was coming from, and he wouldn't want to come out stumbling around in the darkness.

It took the cook a long time to get to bed, in Martin's opinion. Finally, just when the fog seemed thick enough to black out the glowing kitchen window, the light went out.

Martin gave the cook another fifteen minutes to fall asleep in his bed behind the galley.

When the little bugler finally rose to his feet before his tent, even the night birds had fallen silent under the enveloping fog. The world fairly ached for an earth-splitting noise.

Martin Butterfield gave the world what it asked.

He had not watched the mechanical operation of Lawrence Larrabee's lips for nothing. Too, Martin Butterfield had been naturally blessed with a "lip" and a pair of lungs perfectly designed for the task to which he had set himself.

For an instant, the mouthpiece felt cool as he pressed it against his lips. Breathing deeply, closing his eyes, and exhaling with the force of a young Triton rising from the sea, Martin blew his horn.

The bleat that rang over the hills around Major Lake's camp wavered and coursed, vibrating tender green leaves on young maples, shaking pebbles loose on the cliffs, and causing small animals to raise their heads in wonderment.

Before the echoes came satisfyingly back, Martin Butterfield sent another wild call flying and then, with that inexhaustible strength that boys can find for any activity except work, he filled the valley to its rims with a perfect cacophony of bugle sounds.

The sounds had no musical relationship, it is true; but that troubled the bugler not at all. There was plenty of time for learning bugle calls in full detail.

The question now was volume. Martin did not yet know his own strength on the bugle and he intended to measure it, among other pleasurable pursuits.

By the time he took his first rest, which was forced upon him by no weakness of his own but rather by the bubbling condition of his instrument, Martin realized he had underestimated his own strength and overestimated the cook's sleeping abilities.

From the direction of the galley came a voice: "You cut out that unholy racket or I'll . . ."

It was an impressive description, even for an old army man. Martin paused.

He tactfully remained silent and his strategy worked. Mr. Slater retired into the depths of his dark cubicle, slamming the door. Martin waited until the cook got a better and more solid start on his sleeping; it was clearly apparent that the first concert had been a little premature.

When he made his second attack on the bugle, it was altogether the more satisfying for having waited.

Quite by accident, Martin blew a clearly recognizable phrase from the beginning of Taps—three long notes in correct succession.

Thereupon Martin filled the wilderness welkin to overflowing with an ear-splitting fraction of Taps.

Standing before his tent, erect and small in the darkness, it was not hard to see himself on the field of Gettysburg, silhouetted ramrod-straight in his Union blue uniform against the sunset, blowing a tribute to his brave comrades on that historic day.

It was a superb vision. Martin gave vent to his feelings fully through the large end of the bugle.

Bla-a-a—bla—bla-a-a-a-a!

It is possible that he might have struck luckily upon a further phrase of the sunset call if it had not been for Ed Slater, the cook, who seemed to suffer from insomnia just like his father did at home.

Before Martin realized that his position at Gettysburg was under attack, it had been captured by the cook, who reached for the bugle just as the peaceful evening was shaken by a further sound—general threshing noises in the neighboring underbrush followed by a loud clear voice:

"Halloo in the camp there!" Major Lake's voice came. "Will you please let us have another toot on that bugle? We seem to have become—ahem—a little confused in the fog!"

Ed Slater, the old army man, snorted: "He's went and got lost again—only this time he didn't have no horse!"

If ever Martin obeyed both spirit and letter of an order, it was now.

Bla-a-a—bla—bla-a-a-a-a!

The loud beacon of sound brought the major homing like a pigeon.

Before the military figure was visible in the mists, he began awarding decorations and commendations for meritorious conduct on the part of Martin Butterfield.

"Quick thinking, Butterfield, quick thinking, I must say!" the major announced as he came into the circle of light before the tent, a tattered and dampened but still jaunty field commander.

Martin would gladly have foregone the pleasures of the greeting in order to hide Lawrence Larrabee's bugle but he was unable to do so; his worthy hand was tightly gripped by the major's.

The lost-and-found army swarmed around them in the darkness and what might have become an unalloyed triumph for Martin was impaired by the inevitable intrusion.

The intruder was Lawrence Larrabee, whose desire to get at the center of things caused him to step heavily upon the cold, damp toe of Mr. Ed Slater, the cook, a bare toe that had recently been as warm as toast in bed.

Lawrence lost no time in making clear the purpose of his dash to the major's side.

"He stole my bugle, Major," Lawrence shouted ungratefully. "Nobody told him he could blow my bugle."

The major raised his hand with such dignity that even Lawrence was silenced.

"Tut, tut, Larrabee," he said majestically. "Let's not go into technicalities at this time. Martin was only being a good soldier. . . ."

The good soldier grew visibly, though with an air of careless modesty that became his noble little figure.

Lawrence Larrabee retired into an ungracious limbo, muttering to himself like a coward slinking from Gettysburg.

The major rubbed his hands pleasantly. He was really very happy to be back in camp with his valuable little paying guests safe and sound. No telling what might have happened if they had been lost all night—he felt as festive as if he had won a battle in a war.

This spirit of festivity proved too much. "Let's all have something hot to drink and a sandwich or two," he cried. "How about it, cook?"

Now Ed Slater did not mind cooking three meals a day. But he regarded with a certain distaste the business of being hauled out of bed in the middle of the night by a maniac blowing a bugle—and especially a maniac who attracted a whole, unnecessary, hungry army into camp to eat at a time when honest folk were abed. It wouldn't have hurt anything, in Ed Slater's considered opinion, for the whole kit and kaboodle to have stayed lost for one measly night.

But Ed Slater, formerly of the cavalry, was a good soldier.

"Yes, sir, Major," he said.

The soldierly cook stood at attention in bare feet and nightshirt.

"I'm sure," he added, "that Martin Butterfield will be glad to assist with the preparations—and with the dishes."

To the major's surprise, Martin instantly agreed. In the darkness, the major could not discern the degree of encouragement supplied to Martin by Ed Slater's powerful hand resting on his noble little skull.

The hand moved in a twisting circle and Martin did an about-face toward the kitchen.

"We don't want to keep *everybody* up all night, do we, Martin?" Ed Slater inquired sweetly.

"I—" said Martin, but the rest was lost in the sudden motion of marching.

Major Lake heard Ed Slater compliment Martin on his excellent bugle playing as they went off together.

It pleased the major. He stood fondly watching the soldierly little figure beside the soldierly big figure of ex-Corporal Slater.

Camp life does wonderful things to ennoble the spirit and develop the character of small boys. All you have to do, the major reflected, is understand youngsters and sympathize with them.

It was wonderful how quickly he had been able to bring out the best in Martin Butterfield.

CHAPTER 5

The Wonderful Wanderer

No sadness is so short as a boy's sadness. It is a great mistake, however, to assume that the brevity of sadness has any relationship to its intensity.

This fact often leads the grown-up world into large errors when dealing with the world of ten-year-olds or, in other words, the sphere wherein Martin Butterfield operated with continuous vigor and with more stamina than those in authority over him ever anticipated accurately.

Martin Butterfield became sad on his fourth day in camp. Why a blue mood settled over his optimistic nature is easy to explain. He had never been away from home so long before and, the novelty of his new surroundings having worn off, he suddenly considered home. Furthermore, he felt a certain sense of martyrdom, occasioned by his almost continuous presence in the galley washing dishes for Mr. Ed Slater, the cook.

Martin had begun to regard Mr. Slater with not a little of the same sentiment that Eliza once accorded a pack of

The tall youth in crew cut, shorts and not much else, operated on a very direct theory of child psychology. When he concluded preliminary operations, there were three moderated figures lined up before him, figures modified somewhat as a result of the disturbance he had come to quell.

Lawrence Larrabee was altered to the extent of a swelling eye; Martin Butterfield appeared to have been swiped across the countenance by an angry tomcat; Sparky Roberts rubbed a rising knoll on his forehead with a mixture of curiosity and malignant regret.

"One-two-three, start talking," said the counselor with a frostiness born of three summers' experience in the counseling profession.

"He—" began Lawrence.

"He—" repeated Sparky.

"He—" concluded Martin.

At this point, the counselor wound up the taking of testimony.

"Enough," he announced. "All three of you will spend the morning policing up the grounds of the camp."

Now "policing up the grounds" in Major Lake's camp was no mean assignment, the camp comprising some fifty acres of hill, bosky dale and parade ground. The punishment was a fate reserved for extreme misbehavior and was rarely invoked, the assumption being that the camp was peopled by little gentlemen of quality.

Fighting was one famous ground for the penalty.

The pre-breakfast air of the North Outpost was rent with a loud sniffle from Lawrence Larrabee, who had never policed the grounds because he had been a model boy for three summers in camp. There were no sniffles from Martin and Sparky, who had never policed the grounds simply because they hadn't been around long enough to win the distinction until now.

"I'll meet you three fellows by the flagpole after breakfast," said the counselor.

If silence meant assent, the counselor was accorded agreement before he turned on his boondocker's heel and strode authoritatively out of the tent to get Major Lake's confirmation of the sentence.

"I think I'll get moved to another tent," said Lawrence Larrabee not exactly unreasonably.

"Nobody made you come in our tent," replied Martin without reference to the facts of bunk assignments.

"Nobody asked you," added Sparky

"Okay, I *won't* get moved. Yah!" said Lawrence with a kind of logic not uncommon in more learned centers than a boys' camp.

The speed with which boys' moods can change is best demonstrated by the swift conclusion of this conversation when the counselor shouted: "Five minutes till breakfast, everybody!"

Martin Butterfield was the first boy in chow line; Sparky Roberts was second and Lawrence Larrabee was a creditable third as the door of the mess hall swung open to admit what Ed Slater sentimentally called "them hungry hellions."

After the inner man was as adequately provided for as Major Lake's advertisements promised, there followed a period when the outer boy made up his bunk. Then came the moment when Martin Butterfield, Sparky Roberts, and Lawrence Larrabee repaired to the flagpole on the parade ground to counsel with their counselor.

His advice was brief and to the point. The tall young man awarded each party to belligerence a shoulder sack, a cane equipped with a sharp nail on the end, and a rake for heavy duty litter picking.

"Now get to work," he said. "Major Lake will be watching you guys through his office window."

The mood of the three campers had changed again, swiftly and surely, to a feeling of sullen, sorrowful desolation.

"Say," said Lawrence, whose experience in punishment had heretofore been limited to observing the infliction of it on others, "he didn't mean we had to clean up the *whole camp*, did he?"

" 'At's what he said," Martin replied out of the depth of many dismaying school experiences, "and 'at's what he meant."

"Holy smoke!" said Lawrence with such a genuine note of alarm that it reached into his comrades' hearts.

"It ain't so bad, Lawrence," Martin said helpfully.

"Naw," said Sparky. "It don't matter."

They marched off in the bright sun, spearing bits of paper off the turf and raking up handfuls of twigs and other litter.

"Wisht I was home," said Martin. "This camp ain't like if you was a soldier or an Indian chief or—or something."

"We could be swimming in the ole creek right now if we were home," Sparky said wistfully.

"It sure would be nice swimming in old Lick Creek," Lawrence said. This observation was of special interest. When Lawrence was at home he was never allowed to swim in Lick Creek because he might "catch something" in that filthy swimming hole which was natatorially open to everyone equally.

Lawrence's two partners tactfully refrained from mentioning this embarrassingly obvious fact. They acted as if Lawrence had a perfect right to speak as a habitué of Lick Creek.

Speedily does mutual hardship forge out mutual friendship. As previously stated, a boy's sadness is a sudden thing. So also are his loyalties.

Like a span of plowing ponies, the three true friends marched up and down the green parade, savoring the hoops

73

of steel that bound them and presenting a picture of earnest penance for Major Lake to observe through his window.

After three sweeps over the center of the camp, a reconnaissance was in order. The litter pickers discovered that Major Lake was absent now, probably gone to town for the mail. The trio retired over a low rise of land to the farthest end of the camp where they entered the fringe of forest and settled in the shade.

If the young counselor had seen them then, he might have been disappointed in their conduct, but he would also have been hard put to prove that he had ever seen three more sweetly friendly children.

"You got to do too much what people tell you around this camp," Sparky Roberts observed idly as he settled flat on his back under a big maple.

"They don't let you do anything you *want* to do," Martin amplified while he selected a cool, mossy slope on which to recline. "They *make* you do stuff."

"Well," said Lawrence, to whom disagreement with the conventions of society was something new, "it was always run this way before but I never noticed—" Lawrence sank down and began to chew a stalk of sweet grass in meditation.

"That's the trouble with you, Lawrence," Martin said, "you just don't notice stuff."

Lawrence accepted this judgment with the earnest attention of a scholar who would certainly like to get *A* on the final exam.

"It doesn't seem bad when they tell you to do stuff in school," he ventured.

Martin spat in a manner acquired through studious observance of loafers at the Fern Township firehouse at home, and then looked off into the woods where the tender June leaves glittered in patterns of sunshine and shade.

"Why should a camp be run like a school?" he asked.

There was a silence before the reply came. And the reply startled all the boys—not because of what it was but because of where it came from.

A voice from the underbrush, a rasping but friendly voice, said, "A camp sure ought to be different from a school."

The boys were halfway to their feet ready to flee from this ghostly presence when the source heaved into sight from the bushes a few feet away.

A hobo, a gentleman of the road, sat up from what had obviously been his bed for the night and turned a round, merry face upon the three boys. The stranger was bald and his head was sunburned to a fine rich brown that was deepened by a straggly white mustache showing above a set of big teeth.

"Yes, sir," said the hobo, "now that you mention it, I'd say a camp should be a better place than a school."

Sitting there in the bushes, he stretched and yawned.

"A tramp!" whispered Martin Butterfield with true instinct. Martin had never before seen a tramp close up.

The tramp thereupon got to his feet slowly, revealing a small, rotund figure in shabby clothing that was neither black nor brown nor blue nor any color but the dusty, worn, salt-and-pepper hue that only the road and the open countryside can bestow.

Martin Butterfield was suspended in that movement which is exactly halfway between full standstill and full flight.

The tramp, recognizing his state, expertly halted the threatened exodus.

"Let's sit down, men," he said.

"Jumpin' jiminy!" said Sparky Roberts, finding his voice after a brief search.

"Hello," said Lawrence, feeling a certain comfort in the amenities even if prior to sudden flight.

The tramp moved about and rolled up his bed into a small

75

bundle while the boys sat down. Then he sat down cross-legged before them.

"My name's Bill," he said.

Fear began speedily to change into curiosity in three natures that greeted each day as a wholly new and interesting experience. Three rapt faces looked into the face of Bill, meeting a countenance that had no doubt viewed all the wonders of the world. Bill's face underwent a slow diminution of good cheer and a rapid increase of sorrow.

"Somebody here called me a tramp," he murmured unhappily.

Martin Butterfield flushed with embarrassment, and his comrades certified his identity as the culprit by turning and looking upon him reproachfully.

"I don't hold it against you," Bill said. "Naturally I look like a tramp but I'm really a migrant—yes, a migrant, that's what old Bill is."

Curiosity banished Martin's sudden embarrassment. "A what?" he inquired.

"A migrant," Bill repeated. "Old Bill is a migrant, fifty years and more now. A wanderer over the face of the earth, a traveler, you might say. Always on the go and no place to light."

He stroked his bald pate, snuffled heavily and turned to Martin, but Martin beat him to it.

"Haven't you got any home?" Martin asked.

"Nope," said Bill dismally, "I ain't had no home since I got lost from my mammy when I was but a tot of three."

"Man, oh, man!" exclaimed Martin.

"You must have been everywhere and seen everything," said Sparky.

"Do you always sleep in the woods?" inquired the more factually minded Lawrence Larrabee.

"Always," said Bill, nodding his big bald dome slowly so that it glinted brownly in the sun.

"Even when it rains?" inquired Sparky.

"Even when it snows!" replied Bill, thereby beating Martin's question an instant before it was asked.

There was a short period of meditation under the sunlit maple while this information was properly digested.

"I told you fellows *my* name," said Bill. "Now let's see. What are *your* names?"

There were three orderly replies.

"I'm Martin."

"I'm Sparky."

"I'm Lawrence Christopher Larrabee, Junior."

Old Bill rewarded Lawrence's encyclopedic report with interest and then with a slowly growing expression of happy surprise.

"Well, well!" he said, shaking his head. "Imagine that! To think that I—"

There was a quaver in his voice as he broke off. Instead of finishing his remark, he gently patted Lawrence on the head.

Lawrence was mystified and gratified by this special attention, while his comrades were only mystified.

"Imagine what?" asked Martin.

Bill, the migrant, looked down at his crossed legs with great emotion.

"Who'd believe it?" he inquired. "You see, boys, it's just that—well, my name happens to be Bill Christopher Larrabee!"

This astonishing statement hung over the forest glade just long enough for a cloud of doubt no larger than a man's hand to rise on the horizon. Lawrence Larrabee's face reflected that cloud.

But Bill Christopher Larrabee banished it as effectively as a gust of wind drives away a thunderhead.

"Lawrence, my dear boy," he said eagerly, "how is your father, my brother Larry?"

"He's very well, thank you," replied Lawrence with his customary courtesy before he realized that this strange migrant had actually spoken the name of his own father.

"You knew my father's name. . . ." Lawrence murmured wonderingly.

"Of course," Bill said. "Why shouldn't I—my own blood brother?"

Lawrence swallowed hard, seemed to cogitate, waver, and then decide something.

"I just never heard of you, that's all," Lawrence said slowly.

"When I got lost, it was such an awful blow that they don't speak of it no more, I guess," said Bill with humility.

Lawrence looked at Bill Christopher Larrabee with widening awe. Martin and Sparky regarded Lawrence with envy for having discovered such a fine and interesting relative right out here in the woods. Perhaps their envy was the clinching argument. Lawrence could not refuse to accept so fortunate a fate.

"My uncle!" he said thoughtfully. "Imagine finding you . . . after all these years!"

Thus, in the silence of the forest, did Bill Christopher Larrabee become the first migrant ever to climb into the family tree of the Larrabees, a proud structure whose limbs had borne many a judge and senator, professor and rector, but as far as anyone knows, never before a migrant from a hobo jungle.

Bill Christopher Larrabee lost no time in making known the state of his personal welfare to his new-found relative.

"Boy, Lawrence," he said, "am I ever hungry!"

78

Bill's nephew and his nephew's two little friends responded by looking at each other.

"Perhaps the cook would let you have a little something for me," Bill hinted, "or perhaps there might be something lying around that he wouldn't care about."

Feeling the weight of family responsibility, Lawrence finally volunteered for a mission that was to initiate him into the realm of larceny.

It was a tribute to Lawrence's loyalty to home and family perhaps that he was able to return in fifteen minutes with an unbalanced breakfast diet of four stacked cherry pies.

"You're a good boy, nephew," commented Bill Christopher Larrabee.

And Bill proved a generous uncle. He passed the pies around, one to each boy. "It makes a fellow real proud to have a relative who can do things," Bill added as he settled down.

The compliment produced a remarkable result in Lawrence Larrabee.

"There's plenty more where those pies came from, Uncle Bill," he said carelessly.

"Good boy," replied Uncle Bill.

For the second time in an hour, Martin Butterfield and Sparky Roberts were deeply envious of Lawrence Larrabee.

That morning Uncle Bill Christopher proved to be an uncle eminently worth having.

In a mere two hours, he gave the boys a course in woodsmanship that covered more ground than Major Lake's camp taught in a summer, although the lessons differed somewhat from those of the major's recommended program of study.

First, he proceeded to the brook, followed by his three scholars. There he made willow whistles with quick, deft strokes of a knife that was old and worn but as sharp and useful as years of service could make it.

After a tuneful half-hour, Bill commanded silence along the stream while he extracted a little net from his bundle. In a few moments of careful work in a quiet pool, he taught his charges how to net a trout for their supper any time they happened to get caught out at mealtime.

"Look out for the game warden, though," he admonished them.

In a neighboring farmer's pasture he showed them the correct side from which to milk a cow, which he did expertly into a large canteen cup which then passed from mouth to mouth.

"A portable soda fountain for milk shakes," he observed. "The best things in life are free."

In an old orchard where the June fruit was coming ripe, Bill gave a short course in practical botany, with the result that the boys could tell sweet cherries from sour ones without even wasting the effort of tasting before picking a hatful.

Bill also taught them to be as alert as Indians on war patrol against being caught by the farmer.

The morning course of study ended near a farm henhouse about a mile from Major Lake's camp. Bill was about to demonstrate a quick and quiet method of dispatching a tender but noisy hen, when a farm hand appeared at the coop to invite the four visitors to get off the property before a shotgun drove them off.

Bill was philosophical as he made for the road and the woods near the camp.

"This world is just full of soreheads," he said affably.

Altogether it was an entrancing morning whose hours fled unnoticed. The boys and Uncle Bill Christopher were back on the edge of the camp when noon came and the dinner bell rang—in the absence of the usually reliable bugler.

A pall as deep as it was sudden descended over three-fourths of the gathering in the forest glade.

"The major's gonna be mad at us," said Sparky.

"Maybe he forgot about us," suggested Martin.

"I wonder if the cook noticed about the pies—" Lawrence murmured.

Uncle Bill was sympathetic. "It will be all right, boys," he said. "I'm sure everything will be all right—quite!"

Perhaps the note of confidence in his voice did it. Perhaps it was only the common human weakness of falling back upon someone else in time of adversity.

In any case, Uncle Bill's confidence resulted in an idea that suddenly glowed in three minds like a Mazda bulb and hung illuminatingly over the forest glade for a full moment before Martin Butterfield spoke.

"If you would come to lunch with us, Bill," he said with more humility than logic, "maybe Major Lake wouldn't be sore."

Uncle Bill sat up with a startled look. Then his merry little countenance softened into a wry grin, which was succeeded by a mildly speculative twinkle in the eye.

"I ain't got nothing to lose," he chuckled to himself.

"What?" inquired Martin.

"I said I'll be glad to go with you boys," Uncle Bill replied.

Major Lake was seated in lonely grandeur at the camp director's head table, there being no parents or relatives visiting the camp as his luncheon guests that day.

He was mildly irritated at the sudden odd behavior of the Larrabee boy, who, it seemed, had fallen quite unexpectedly upon evil ways. He was turning a theory over in his mind, even as he turned over the roast beef on his plate, that perhaps that Butterfield lad had something to do with Larrabee's troubles.

It was unlikely that a youngster of Larrabee's background would get into trouble unassisted.

The major was a thorough believer in family and tradition, especially families who had a tradition of sending their young offspring to camp every summer.

It was now five minutes past twelve, and Major Lake's military mustaches twitched irritably as he looked over the buzzing mess hall where his boys were energetically eating. His gaze paused at the table where four chairs stood empty —three of them belonging to campers and the fourth belonging to the counselor conducting a search of grounds and woods at this moment.

Major Lake did not have to wait long for an explanation of the absences.

While his gaze roved over his domain, the screen door opened and the counselor, his young face shining with perspiration and agitation, entered and made straight for the major.

"Well, Haskins," said the major with the faintest suggestion of a question.

"Sir," said Haskins, the counselor, "I found 'em—they're out on the porch . . ."

"Bring them in instantly," ordered the major crisply.

"Sir," Haskins went on hesitantly, "there's a man with them—Larrabee says it's his uncle."

"Uncle!" ejaculated the major. "Why didn't you say so in the first place, Haskins? Bring him in." The major did not pause to brook any more conversation. Instead he turned toward the kitchen and called, "Slater!"

Slater, who had been observing this tête-a-tête with as much interest as everybody else in the hall, had also managed to hear all of it. He surprised the major by appearing instantly, carrying four plates and setting places for the boys and their guest at the head table before Major Lake could order him to do so.

"Always on the spot, Slater," the major observed with wry satisfaction.

It pleased him to feel that Lawrence's uncle would no doubt notice how efficiently run was the establishment of a former military man; how well prepared for any contingency.

The major was so engrossed in observing Slater's handi-work that he didn't see Uncle Bill Christopher Larrabee until that personage, with his dusty and threadbare suit, collarless shirt and florid countenance, was grinning toothily down upon the excellent crockery and cutlery of the head table.

Ranged beside him were, in order: Lawrence Larrabee, Martin Butterfield and Sparky Roberts.

The major looked at Uncle Bill—then looked again. He was sufficiently nonplused not to rise from his seat.

"Wha—" he said, and it will never be known whether the lonely syllable was simply an exclamation or the beginning of a question that Major Lake deemed it wise to omit.

Lawrence Larrabee, supported by the presence of his uncle, beamed on the major.

"I wish to present my uncle," he said in his best preparatory school manner, "Mr. Bill Christopher Larrabee."

The certainty with which he pronounced that impressive name was enough to give any doubter pause, including Major Lake. The boy *must* know his own uncle.

After all, even the Larrabee clan could have a black sheep or a practical joker somewhere in its widespread boughs; better names had been beclouded by their bearers, though Major Lake could not think of a cloudier case at the moment than this Larrabee that stood before him.

"How do you do, sir," he said, rising with the same stanch courage that had sent him out of the trenches in '17.

"Howdy," said Bill Christopher, extending a hand that was worn with grime, if not with toil.

"I wasn't expecting any of Lawrence's—" the major began.

Bill Christopher was nothing if not magnanimous about his unexpected arrival as a guest.

"Neither was I," he said cheerily, "but the boys wanted me to see the place and so I came. Hope it don't trouble you too much, Maje, old boy."

Maje, old boy, summoned up his self-control again.

"Won't you be seated?" he said.

There was a scraping of chairs that underscored the silence throughout the dining room as a hundred pair of eyes curiously, and discourteously, inspected the most interesting Larrabee ever seen anywhere.

The major tapped his glass with a knife. "Everyone will eat his lunch, please," he ordered precisely.

Everyone thereupon pretended to, while Bill Christopher tucked a napkin under his chin.

The major inspected Lawrence Larrabee, but that bright, benign countenance told him nothing except that it had been recently struck a blow in the eye. Could it be possible that Lawrence was telling a lie? the major asked himself. He consulted the truly admirable little Lawrence's countenance again. It could not be, the major decided.

The major then studied the less admirable faces of Martin Butterfield and Sparky Roberts. Martin and Sparky returned his gaze shyly and then cast their eyes down upon the food that the cook was placing before them.

Martin's face said clearly, "We ain't done anything, I don't think."

The major nodded to Martin. "I wish to see you after lunch, Butterfield," he said.

"Me, sir?" asked Martin.

The major did not waste further attention on him. He turned to Uncle Bill Christopher Larrabee.

"How long do you plan to stay with us?" he asked hesitantly.

"Oh," said Bill, "I'll have to go right after lunch."

This statement brightened Major Lake's outlook immeasurably.

"Shame you can't stay—" he said jovially.

Martin Butterfield, Lawrence Larrabee, and Sparky Roberts looked up at Uncle Bill simultaneously. Not stay for a while?

"Say, Bill," Martin said, "we got plenty of room up at the North Outpost for another cot in our tent."

Bill Christopher looked up from diligent work over a large slice of beef.

"That's mighty fine of you, Martin," he said, "mighty fine."

The major cleared his throat. "Of course, the boys would be happy to have you," he said, "but we really can't have more than three in a tent—rule of the camp, you know."

"Quite all right," replied Bill with a twinkle, "I wouldn't mind a little crowding, if you know what I mean."

"That's swell," said Martin.

Major Lake seemed to lose whatever remained of his appetite.

He looked at the odd figure sitting there at his table. He hoped that no other visitors would descend upon him today while this creature was present. Looking at the heavily damaged clothing, the major wondered whether Mr. Bill Christopher Larrabee had possibly been in an accident of

85

some kind to cause so much destruction to his attire. He wondered what Mr. Larrabee's profession might be.

And he might have inquired, except that at that moment the major received another unexpected guest.

The door to the mess hall opened long enough to reveal a station wagon glittering in the bright sunlight outside. When the door closed behind a large incoming female figure, Major Lake realized that he was about to receive the majestic personage of Mrs. Lawrence Christopher Larrabee Senior.

Lawrence Junior, however, had seen her first.

"Mother!" he piped in a voice pierced with delight.

"Lawrence!" the tall, buxom blond lady cried. They met and embraced halfway across the hall before Mrs. Larrabee took inventory of her offspring.

"Lawrence!" she cried again, but this time it didn't sound like the same exclamation. "Your eye! It's all black. And your clothes, they look simply—simply disgusting! Lawrence, you poor dear!"

Her small soiled son backed away from these embarrassing female fulminations in public.

"Mother," he said quietly, "I've got a surprise for you!"

When Mother turned to accompany him to the head table, it struck her forcefully that Major Lake was choosing odd luncheon company lately. Lawrence pulled her toward the stranger but she steered straight for the camp director.

"Major," she murmured with a politeness fringed with icicles. She put out her hand.

The major rose, momentarily searching for his voice which seemed to have got lost. He smiled tentatively, reconsidered and looked stern, reconsidered again and simply looked flabbergasted, which was his real state in the first place.

He glanced uneasily at Mrs. Larrabee, who promptly stared him down.

He glanced at his other guest. More properly, he glanced at the spot where his other guest had just been. Mr. Bill Christopher Larrabee was no longer at his plate and place.

Snatching up a piece of beef for later reference at some more peaceable, and distant, point, Uncle Bill Christopher Larrabee was at this very instant taking leave of Major Lake's camp for boys. He was already halfway to the door, and by the time Major Lake recovered his voice Uncle Bill had passed through the door of the mess hall and into the great outdoors that is the home of all migrants.

"Stop, thief!" Major Lake shouted illogically.

The departing apparition continued across the porch at high speed while fascinated eyes followed him.

At the cry of "thief!" Mrs. Larrabee drew her son protectively toward her. But Lawrence was in no mood for protection. He wriggled free and made for the door in pursuit of his distance-consuming uncle.

"Hey, Uncle Bill," he piped dismally, "where are you goin', Uncle Bill?"

There was a silence while Mrs. Larrabee digested the meaning of this cry. Uncle! Uncle indeed!

She stared at her son silhouetted in the doorway peering out into the sunshine.

"Uncle?" she cried. "Did you address that—that man as uncle?"

"Sure," Lawrence said without turning. "He's the one that got lost when he was three. That was him all right. And now we went and scared him away—" Lawrence was near to tears.

Perhaps it might be expected that Mrs. Larrabee would have been angry at Lawrence for his error. Women, alas, are not so constructed.

87

Mrs. Larrabee turned, instead, to a better victim, Major Lake.

"Did you think for a minute—" she whispered with a certain ferocity.

The major cleared his throat. "Apparently," he said, "I must have been misled."

Few truths have ever been so mildly stated.

And still fewer have produced so adverse an effect.

For a moment Mrs. Larrabee suffered what appeared to be a severe attack of strangulation.

"You mean, Major, that you thought that—that—that character was Lawrence's uncle?"

A more precise description of what the major had thought could hardly have been drawn. The major replied, "Oh, no, no, my dear Mrs. Larrabee. How could you —"

However, the major's sly change of heart, it developed, was not shared unanimously among the other guests at the head table, a knot that now included the returning Lawrence.

"He ran away," Lawrence said in a stunned tone, looking first at his mother and then at his two small comrades.

Martin and Sparky stared deeply at Lawrence. They understood. They sympathized. They grieved with Lawrence, bereft, as he was, of the only wholly interesting and admirable relative he had ever had.

"Maybe we could go up in the woods where your uncle lives and ask him to come back," Martin suggested.

Martin did not understand why Mrs. Larrabee suddenly needed a chair for support any more than he understood why he and his two comrades were immediately excused from lunch by Major Lake.

Outside in the sun, sitting on the edge of the mess-hall porch, the three boys waited while the major made certain explanations to Mrs. Larrabee.

"When I grow up," Martin announced decisively, "I'm gonna be a bum, Lawrence, just like your Uncle Bill Christopher."

"Me, too," Sparky said.

Lawrence Larrabee considered a moment, then said, "Maybe I shall, too—for a while at least."

Unfortunately, this conversation was overheard inside the mess hall. Unfortunately for Martin, it could not have come at a more opportune time for Major Lake's purposes.

"I'm sure," said the sharp-eared Major Lake to the equally sharp-eared Mrs. Larrabee, "that none of the blame for this incident rests on Lawrence."

Mrs. Lawrence Christopher Larrabee Senior could and did agree, as only a mother of a son in trouble knows how.

The boys sat on the edge of the porch, oblivious of all but the disappearance of their new friend.

Their mood of deep companionship, rooted in commiseration, lasted exactly until the moment when Martin and Sparky were brusquely dispatched to resume their litter gathering while Lawrence was sent happily to rest period and then to the swimming pool with the more respectable elements of the camp.

The distant vision of cool water splashing and brown bodies flashing in the sun worked a remarkable change of spirit in Martin Butterfield and his accomplice. By the time they returned to the North Outpost at 5:00 P.M., the very conditions that had produced their early morning offense against society had been reëstablished.

With one alteration—which was discovered by the two outlaws when they burst into their tent looking for that Stinker Larrabee.

Lawrence's bunk was empty. He had foresightedly packed his worldly camping goods and moved to a safer tent.

Martin and Sparky observed the vacant cot contemplatively.

"Well," sighed Sparky, "we don't have him to bother us no more anyway."

"Him?" sniffed Martin. "We should have known that stinker couldn't have a real, genuine bum for an uncle."

Martin lay down on his cot and looked at his friend. "Wisht I was home, Sparky," he said.

The day had come full cycle.

CHAPTER 6

Genius, Junior Grade

EARLY in the morning of his fifth day in camp, Martin Butterfield voluntarily wrote his parents a letter. The letter expressed fond hope that he would soon have concluded his camping in "this awful place."

Early in the evening of his fifth day in camp, Martin voluntarily wrote his parents a second letter. The letter informed them that he had won the 50-yard swimming sprint championship of the camp and he sure did like this camp and he sure was glad he was here.

Martin was not troubled by the possibility that these two letters might have sounded contradictory to the casual reader. By the time he got around to writing the second one, he had forgotten his attitude in the first.

His parents, being his parents, probably surmised that fact.

In any case, Martin's homesickness ended on the fifth day. On or about that same day, most of the homesickness that had swept over other inmates of the establishment like an epidemic seemed to vanish as mysteriously as it had come.

By the sixth day in camp, Martin Butterfield found no pain in his surroundings. If it can be assumed that a boy is happy when he is not in rebellion against his environment, then it can be said that Martin Butterfield was happy thereafter.

Certainly his appetite was excellent on the morning of his twelfth day in camp. He ate a bowl of oatmeal, three slices of toast, two eggs, two fat sausages, and a dish of prunes. The fact that he consumed prunes of his own free will is perhaps the best gauge of Martin's contentment; at home, he faced them only occasionally and then under powerful parental duress.

In the chair beside Martin, Sparky Roberts matched him egg for egg, sausage for sausage, and prune for prune.

The table conversation was extremely limited, for the utilitarian reason that there was no purpose in wasting energy on talk while more important matters hung fire.

It was only as the morning pangs became heavily dulled that boys' voices began to rise in the dining hall and other interests superseded dying hunger.

Martin Butterfield turned to his friend and gave voice to a rumor he had heard in the washroom earlier in the morning and which he had been saving for some such dull period as was now descending.

"I heard we were going to take up finger painting this morning," he said.

"What?" inquired Sparky Roberts with that precise note of curiosity Martin Butterfield hoped for and, in fact, had earlier expressed himself when he had heard this cryptic announcement while brushing his teeth.

"Yep, that's what I heard," Martin said. "We're gonna take up finger painting today."

Sparky Roberts looked at his friend and frankly admitted his ignorance.

"What's finger painting?" he asked.

"Don't you know what finger painting is?" Martin countered.

"You don't either," Sparky retorted.

"Okay, then, I guess you don't want to find out what finger painting is."

"What is it then?"

"Well," said Martin, delivering himself of the information he had acquired only an hour before, "it's painting with your fingers."

Sparky Roberts looked at Martin in candid disappointment.

"That's the craziest thing I heard of yet," he said.

Since this was a very apt description of Martin's own feeling on the subject, Martin's air of superiority melted.

"That's what I think," he admitted. "Who wants to mess around with their fingers in picture paint?"

Messing around with any other kind of paint was a perfectly honorable pursuit; it was axiomatic that the elders of the Butterfield and Roberts households always disposed of old house paint cans lest their heirs find them and put the scrapings to spectacular use.

The two boys considered the subject of finger painting in silence for a moment before the major's little bell tinkled, releasing them to the outdoors.

Martin and Sparky passed through the door, leaving all thought of finger painting until such time as the world forced the subject upon them.

Outside in the sun, the green parade ground boiled with the freshly released breakfasters and Martin and Sparky were seized with a fever that demanded pushing, shoving, punching and tugging at one's fellows, a great deal of running and leaping, and above all, loud noises emitted at a monotonously large volume.

In the midst of this activity, few of the campers took note of a sleek gray convertible coupé that slid up to the door of the dining hall. After it was parked, they all took notice of it, however.

In the red leather seat, next to the lady driver, sat a beautiful little girl, with hair that shone black in the sun. Driver and passenger were dressed exactly alike as far as the campers could see, both wearing plaid sport shirts of some glistening, light material.

By the time the pair debarked, it was evident that the resemblance went even further. Both were wearing blue jeans and high-heeled cowboots of delicate tan leather.

The noise on the parade ground subsided as the woman and the child passed around the car and up the steps of the dining hall, disappearing into the depths of the building. They were obviously on their way to see Major Lake.

"What's an old girl doing in this camp?" Sparky Roberts muttered.

"Yeah," said someone else. "Who told her she could come?"

Martin shared the general disapprobation of little girls and women, whether in the camp or in the world at large.

It was not until morning assembly on the parade ground that the problem of the mysterious presences was solved. Major Lake introduced Mrs. Barton-Scott and her daughter Emily, announcing that the former was going to teach finger painting this morning to anyone who wished to learn. Those who did not crave such learning could go to the usual classes in woodsmanship and other crafts.

By the most curious of coincidences, each of which could be carefully explained, every boy in the camp reported to the dining hall at 10:00 A.M. for finger-painting class. The long tables were as crowded as if Joe Louis had been present to teach counter-punching with the right hand.

94

The little girl with the jet black hair sat haughtily in a chair up front while her mother went into the mysterious whorls and daubs of color on paper that constitute making pictures with digits and paint.

But if the attention of the room full of potential artists had been exclusively devoted to little Emily when Mrs. Barton-Scott began her lecture on finger painting, it can be said for Mrs. Barton-Scott's effectiveness that the students' attention was at least divided by the time the lecture was finished.

With something of the movements of a magician, Mrs. Barton-Scott tacked up a large sheet of white paper on the board of an easel. Then, using a small palette of primary colors, she began swiftly to "mess things up," as she described it.

Mrs. Barton-Scott was, by the standards of the campers, awful old; she was at least as old as Martin's mother, approaching her mid-thirties. But she was not at all like a schoolteacher. Martin Butterfield subconsciously gave her a good mark for that, although he may have been prejudiced by the presence of her comrade in jeans; he gave *her* a good mark consciously; even Miss Georgianna Semple of the fourth grade in Fern Township, hitherto the apex of all American womanhood as far as Martin was concerned, seemed to diminish in memory.

Martin stared in frank wonder at Emily Barton-Scott sitting in front of dozens of campers, as composed as a veteran actress, which in a way she was. She had sat before many youthful audiences just so, while her mother lectured. She had developed a technique of sitting—with credit to her mother and to herself—and she enjoyed it.

Mrs. Barton-Scott's voice fell in a musical ripple over the hushed hall. It provided a pleasant background for Martin's musings.

While Emily's large dark eyes passed unheeding over him, Martin drifted off into a wonderful world where *he* heedlessly ignored Emily Barton-Scott while he performed a series of feats that brought unidentified thousands to their feet shouting: "Martin Butterfield! Martin Butterfield!"

In those golden moments Martin Butterfield hit a home run in Yankee Stadium, he scored a touchdown in the Rose Bowl, he thundered across the Indianapolis speedway with the checkered flag dazzling his vision, he landed his jet job under the very noses of Admiral Halsey and a black-haired maiden on an aircraft carrier that the admiral had said couldn't handle it, he . . .

What more he would have accomplished in the next few moments must remain a mystery forever, because Martin suddenly felt a sharp nudge in the ribs from Sparky Roberts, sitting beside him.

Martin came to life with sufficient speed to whisper hoarsely, "You cut that out, Sparky, or I'll —"

Sparky looked at him and then nodded his head desperately toward Mrs. Barton-Scott, who was looking at Martin as if she expected something of him. The whole room, Martin realized, had its eyes on him as fully as any of the larger audiences before which he had just been performing.

With a tightening in the throat, quite unlike his feelings in Yankee Stadium, he realized that even little Emily was now looking at him, looking at him with a curious little superior kind of smile, as if she were a grown-up and he were a baby.

Martin instantly hated her—in the same way that spurned young swains develop instantaneous hatred and then, oddly enough, redouble the pursuit.

Martin flushed deeply.

"Didn't you hear?" inquired Mrs. Barton-Scott. "Have we been daydreaming, Mr.—uh—Mr.—what is your name?"

96

Martin rose stiffly from his chair. "Martin Butterfield," he said gruffly.

"Well, come on up, Martin," Mrs. Barton-Scott said. "Don't be bashful."

Martin understood then that he was being brought forward as some kind of partner in a demonstration that he could very well do without. It occurred to him that Mrs. Barton-Scott wasn't any better than a teacher after all.

Silently, with a certain air of embarrassed rebellion, he moved forward. Having heard none of the previous lecture, he was now prepared for an undefined worst. It promptly happened.

Mrs. Barton-Scott laid her hand femininely on his shoulder right in front of everybody, including little Emily, happily dangling her high-heeled cowboots against the rungs of her chair.

Martin promptly wriggled free.

"Now," said Mrs. Barton-Scott, "we'll show how easy it is to make a picture."

Sharing no such intention whatever, Martin was struck dumb.

Meanwhile, with that love of sport that is characteristic of all boys, the entire roster of the camp focused its attention on him, reflecting approximately the same anticipatory cheer they would have given the announcement that a few martyrs were about to be fed to the lions.

Martin mentally noted for later reference the face of Sparky Roberts shining with a certain aspect of disaster hoped-for. Martin also recorded the face of Master Stinker Larrabee for placement well up on his list of intended targets.

He would have made further observations, except that Mrs. Barton-Scott obscured his view while she removed the moonlight scene she had painted with her forefinger

97

and thumb and put up another sheet of paper on which Martin Butterfield was now to work.

"All right, Martin," she said, "now we have a nice clean sheet of paper and here is the palette of paints."

She forced the palette upon his unwilling thumb and Martin stood regarding her with dumbness born of helplessness.

The room rustled with good humor.

"If it isn't more quiet," Mrs. Barton-Scott said, "I'll have someone else up here to help me."

Martin's hopes rose briefly and exploded. Silence fell over the room.

"What would you like to paint, Martin?" she inquired pleasantly.

Martin's desires were distinctly limited in number, but he was reluctant to say as much. Martin had learned that truthfulness, in the wrong place, is only its own reward.

He looked at Mrs. Barton-Scott and then at her daughter and then at the audience.

Mrs. Barton-Scott was not to be denied.

"Let me see," she said, "let's paint a barn."

For lack of anything else to say, Martin heard himself mutter politely, "Yes, ma'am, a barn."

In a spasm of embarrassment, he glanced futilely toward Emily Barton-Scott, whose eyes were now on his every movement.

In blind self-immolation, he reached for the colors on the palette and stirred his finger in the nearest pool of creamy paint. It was a bright blue.

"A barn," Martin murmured hopelessly. Before he could daub the paper with his blue finger, however, Mrs. Barton-Scott halted him.

"Blue, Martin?" she inquired. "Barns aren't blue, are they?"

The class murmured and Stinker Larrabee informed the world in a hoarse whisper that anybody knows barns are red.

Mrs. Barton-Scott looked at Martin. Rebellion was clearly beginning to simmer in her little pupil.

"*Some* barns," Martin said, "are red. Other barns are blue. My grandfather's barn is blue." Martin's grandfather would have been surprised to know that he had suddenly acquired any kind of barn.

"Of course," Mrs. Barton-Scott said, "you can make your barn blue in that case."

An admiring glance from a chair just beyond Mrs. Barton-Scott gave Martin Butterfield an enormous injection of confidence.

Thus strengthened, Martin raised his finger to the pristine sheet of paper and was astonished to discover that his finger made a very interesting blue whorling design at the point where he tentatively placed it. He drew a straight line that was to be his roof pole, a long blue smear that was full of smaller wavy lines.

Finger painting, Martin discovered, had its possibilities. His conviction was confirmed when he lifted his finger and found that he had automatically made an intricate little whorl.

Martin began to feel that possibly he was as gifted in finger painting as in other activities in which he had hitherto taken considerable pride, such as licking Stinker Larrabee.

He was pained by an interruption from Mrs. Barton-Scott. "Hold it right there, Martin," she said.

Martin held it, glancing around at Emily. He smiled vaguely at her.

Emily concentrated her gaze primly on the line he had drawn on the paper and gave the sternest kind of attention to her mother's explanation.

Martin was permitted to continue with his painting only after further instruction about the amount of paint on the finger, the method of turning the finger and thumb, and other tedious details. He was interrupted again. And then again and again.

He never did complete the barn. Far from feeling embarrassed now, he felt that he had been invited up front only to be prevented from showing his skill.

There was one recompense, however, before he was sent back to his chair with a clean sheet of paper to begin painting with the rest of the class.

The last time he looked at Emily and smiled, she smiled shyly back at him. Her smile was full of meaning. Martin translated that smile to suit his own ardent wishes and was, by a system of personal reasoning no faultier than that employed by greater minds, gratified to imagine himself an object of much admiration in certain quarters.

By the time clean sheets of paper had been passed up and down the tables for all campers to begin work, this idea had become a conviction.

If his spectacular blue barn, barely begun up front, had attracted attention, he would now show Miss Emily Barton-Scott what he really could do.

Boxes of paint were distributed from a case in the front of the room and when all potential Rembrandts were ready, Mrs. Barton-Scott made an announcement.

"After we're finished," she said, "we'll hang our paintings along that wall with thumbtacks . . ."

She pointed to the wall near the door where Major Lake was standing now, smiling his benign approval of his guest instructress as well as his group of model campers.

"—and then," she continued enthusiastically, "we'll have a nice surprise. Monsieur Lorenzo Picciotti, the painter, is coming to say hello to us and we'll just ask him to have a look at our work."

Her enthusiasm, however, was not fully reciprocated. A great painter, among the campers, was not so welcome as, say, a great baseball player.

Mrs. Barton-Scott looked disappointed, her eyelashes dropping for a moment, but only for a moment.

"Perhaps," she said, hopefully glancing toward Major Lake, "we could give a little prize to the boy whose painting is considered the best by Monsieur Picciotti."

Major Lake nodded reluctantly. "We'll give the painter of the best picture," he said firmly, "a new dollar bill."

He appeared to believe that newness had something to do with gold content.

The dollar drew a good deal more response than had the name of Monsieur Picciotti, whose work hung in various museums of modern art.

Martin Butterfield, for one, had no objections at all to winning a dollar while he also won plaudits for himself from Miss Emily Barton-Scott.

He was engaged in profound gazing in Emily's direction when Sparky Roberts interrupted his reverie.

"What are you gonna paint, Martin?" whispered Sparky sarcastically. "Another blue barn like your poor old grandpa has?"

Sparky Roberts was the single person in the entire audience who was acutely acquainted with the fact that neither of Martin's grandfathers owned any kind of barn, much less a blue one.

"You're just mad 'cause you didn't get a chance," Martin replied blandly.

Sparky accepted this criticism silently.

"What're you gonna draw?" he persisted.

Martin said, "Don't you wisht you knew?"

He sat gazing steadily at Emily, who was still sitting sublimely in her chair in the front of the room while her mother passed out the last of the paintboxes.

When Mrs. Barton-Scott had finished this chore, she announced that all painters could proceed to paint and that she would pass up and down the rows assisting them. It was then that Emily Barton-Scott slipped down from her seat. She, too, it seemed, would look over the shoulders of the young artists.

This was just such a bonus as Martin Butterfield might have prayed for.

He bent over his paper and began work.

If a blue barn had created a minor sensation, Martin was now prepared to outdo himself by carefully pursuing his theory to its logical end.

In short, he began a painting of a green horse covered with square purple spots eating out of a field of crimson grass under a black sun.

Martin's skill at draftsmanship was something less than his appetite for attracting attention. But he could draw an animal that was recognizably the shape of a horse; it is hardly a compliment to remark that the rest of the details of his picture were up to this standard.

He had only begun to trace out the horse with a heavy green finger when Sparky Roberts, darkly struggling for a hold on Inspiration, leaned over and peered at the art work rapidly being fingered out by his friend.

"What's 'at?" he inquired.

"A horse," said Martin calmly. "Don't you know what a horse looks like?"

"A green horse?" Sparky ejaculated.

"Sure," said Martin, "my grandfather has a green horse —right in his blue barn!"

Such a frontal attack on a potential scoffer achieved its hoped-for measure of surprise and a silence followed.

Sparky shook his head and prepared for work. He began to draw a conventional brown house with a green tree standing in the dooryard.

Throughout the mess hall, heads were bent over the dining tables and fingers moved less than adroitly. Meanwhile Mrs. Barton-Scott and Emily moved along the rows.

Mrs. Barton-Scott would look over one shoulder while Emily would stand on tiptoe and peer over the other. Mrs. Barton-Scott would make some comment: ". . . a little lighter on the paint . . . I'll show you how . . . why not try a nice red here . . ."

Emily would look on in solemn, silent beauty and all eyes around her would watch for some vague sign of approbation.

Martin Butterfield was not unaware of this tour through the potential artists. He concentrated powerfully on speed, if not on quality, in order that his painting would be finished by the time it would meet the eyes of Mrs. Barton-Scott and her daughter.

Thus the greenest horse ever seen in Major Lake's camp came into being. The effect was so startling that Martin himself was a little disappointed at his effort. Whereas a blue barn had seemed only surprising, he now found a verdant horse decorated with square purple patches to be a little unconvincing.

"That's the awfulest thing I ever saw," Sparky Roberts said in a quick appraisal.

Martin scanned Sparky's house.

"Not even an old ghost would live in that thing," he countered.

He returned his gaze to his own work and began to study a possible method of toning it down by adding some brown to his animal, which appeared to be grazing on a sea of flame.

He had not yet plotted out a cure when Mrs. Barton-Scott arrived at Sparky's place.

She glanced at Sparky's house.

"Why, that's a nice house," she said pleasantly. "Look at it, Emily."

Emily looked.

"It's very nice," she said sweetly.

While a rapier of pain pierced Martin's heart, he watched Emily smile traitorously upon Sparky Roberts.

Furthermore, he suffered a deep misgiving. If just any old plain brown house could win this maiden's approval, wasn't it possible that she might dislike a green horse?

He had no time to consider. For reasons that are self-apparent, Mrs. Barton-Scott's attention was drawn from Sparky's brown house by the colored uproar near by.

Silently she reached out and took the paper, but her face lacked any of the kind of surprise that Martin had expected. Instead there was a kind of puzzled wonderment written there.

"Where did you get this idea?" she inquired.

Martin said, "I thought it up."

"Oh," said Mrs. Barton-Scott.

Her daughter, rising to her full height, peeked at the picture.

"Oh!" she gasped. "I never saw anything like that before, Mother."

Her mother smiled sympathetically. "Well . . ." she began.

Martin stole a furtive glance at Emily. He smiled with a certain practiced air of shyness that he had observed in the behavior of Mr. Gene Autry each time the cowboy brought down another rustler.

"It's not so good," he offered, " 'cause I didn't have much time to work."

This remark fell upon the eagerly listening ears of, among others, Sparky Roberts.

"You had as long as anybody else," Sparky observed realistically.

Emily giggled. The bell-like little sound from her throat was the signal for a murmur of derisive comment up and down the table—derisive and potentially hilarious.

Martin Butterfield tried to shrink in size in his chair but he only succeeded in sinking so that his chin was level with the table top.

He remained, however, defiant of the world at large.

"I want my picture back," he said loudly.

Mrs. Barton-Scott looked startled, handed him his picture, and drew her giggling daughter away to view the next picture down the line, a very precise work of art, showing a sunset between two hills that were adorned with triangular spruce trees. Lawrence Larrabee, the artist, waited expectantly; *he* never drew any silly pictures like some people did.

Unfortunately for Lawrence, his expectations, whatever they were, were never fulfilled.

At that moment, a large figure loomed in the doorway of the mess hall. Mrs. Barton-Scott gave a delighted little cry and Monsieur Lorenzo Picciotti, the painter, entered.

Martin Butterfield's reflections upon his own painting were instantly dissolved in more interesting matters.

Monsieur Picciotti was a small boy's delight in every respect.

He rushed to Mrs. Barton-Scott and pecked her on both cheeks as if she were a French aviator getting a medal or something.

He swept up Emily's small white hand and, bending, gave it a courtly kiss.

He bellowed, "My dears, my dears!" repeatedly and then he shook Major Lake's hand so vigorously that the old soldier appeared to suffer from palsy.

But these were only minor details of interest.

The dominating facts about this large man standing near the door were much more fascinating. He wore a spade beard, black as jet; his heavy, flowing locks poured out from beneath a bright red beret; finally, and wonderfully, he wore a monocle which he kept popping in and out of his cavernous right eye socket.

At that moment in history, Martin Butterfield began to amend his purposes in life to include the goal of becoming a great painter. Tentatively, he felt in his pockets for a coin that might be useful in practicing that trick with a monocle. He had no coins.

"Ain't that sumpin'!" he sighed.

Sparky Roberts said, "Can he really see through that eyeglass?"

"That's a moniker, you dumb-bell!" replied Martin.

"Where do you get 'em?" murmured Sparky.

"If you find a pair of glasses with one glass busted, I bet . . ." began Martin.

Martin was interrupted by the sudden attention-clapping of Mrs. Barton-Scott's hands.

"Now, everybody," she said, "this is Monsieur Picciotti. He is willing to judge the pictures but he is a very, very busy gentleman and he hasn't much time, you know."

While Major Lake and Monsieur Picciotti made mutually curious inspections of each other, the boys received their instructions. Each would tack his own picture on the wall immediately.

The bedlam that ensued along the wall may have caused Major Lake to feel a pang of nostalgia for the days of the cavalry charges.

The shoving, pushing, healthy combat was hardly cleared up and Martin's picture had hardly begun to illuminate the whole wall before Monsieur Picciotti's voice surged through the room.

"The green horse!" he cried. "Who is it the artist please?"

The big figure in the red beret, black beard and monocle took a position before the picture. He turned and interrogated the class with a dark, questioning gaze.

Martin Butterfield once more attempted unsuccessfully to shrink in size.

He felt the hot and cold chills of dozens of glances passing over his person.

Miss Emily Barton-Scott looked brightly expectant, her pretty little face flushed and her dark eyes sparkling. Her voice suddenly rang out like a bell.

"Martin did it," she said accusingly.

"Girls!" Martin muttered to himself. He had been right in the first place about girls.

Darkly ruminating on what he would do to the entire world when he got a little bigger, Martin finally responded to a command from Major Lake.

He stood up.

Monsieur Lorenzo Picciotti eyed him through the monocle. Then, as if distrusting the glass, he removed it to inspect the small artist with naked eye.

"Tiens, tiens, tiens!" ejaculated Monsieur Picciotti and then as if to demonstrate his mastery of international exclamation: "Heavens to Betsy!"

Martin was able to stand up under this withering hail chiefly because he was concentrating his mind upon plans for what he would do to Sparky Roberts and Lawrence Larrabee as soon as he got outside.

"Come forward, my fine little man," commanded Monsieur Picciotti.

Martin rose to the occasion. He glared at Sparky and then at Lawrence Larrabee and then at Miss Emily Barton-Scott, and went forward.

When, finally, he stood before the towering figure of Monsieur Picciotti he felt as small as if he were gazing at a cliff above.

Monsieur Picciotti pointed to the painting.

"This is the brilliant conception," he said. "This is the complicated impression!"

It sounded about as bad as Martin had feared it would.

He wilted. "I didn't mean to—" he heard himself say in a small squeak.

Monsieur Picciotti clapped him mightily on the shoulder.

"It is the original and wonderful idea!" he shouted.

Martin Butterfield stiffened and gazed at the large head above him.

He turned and stared at Mrs. Barton-Scott, who stared back.

Martin was fortified. He looked at Emily, while a rapidly growing curiosity blossomed quickly into a question aimed at the huge figure beside him.

"You think it's okay?" he inquired.

"You are the surrealist!" said Monsieur Picciotti. He bent over and, just as if Martin also were a French aviator, pecked him briskly on either cheek.

The surrealist did not fully comprehend what it was that he had suddenly become. But he understood pretty clearly that he had emerged creditably.

He looked with a growing renewal of affection at his painting of the green horse upon the wall.

He was not the only one whose opinion underwent a certain degree of amendment from low to high.

Major Lake came forward with the new dollar bill as promised.

"I don't know much about art," he mumbled, "but I'm glad to present the prize to Martin."

Martin found himself shaking hands with the major.

Mrs. Barton-Scott developed a sudden appreciation of Martin's art.

"You have a very individual style, Martin," she said, "a very personal style, I might say."

The visiting painter boomed approval of this keen perception, this approval of *his* approval. "You say it exactly right, my dear lady," he roared. "He has the *personal* style."

The artist with a personal style only said, "Thank you."

He stood there indecisively for a moment, waiting. He did not wait in vain.

Little Emily Barton-Scott was led forward by her mother.

"The green horse is very nice, Martin," she said prettily.

Martin flushed modestly, not altogether without awareness that it is becoming in a conqueror to blush occasionally.

"Thank you, Emily," he replied.

His conduct was so modest and yet so forthright that even Major Lake was impressed.

The major glanced again at the picture of the green animal on the wall. As an old cavalryman, he realized that he knew much about horses and nothing about art.

He looked ponderously at Martin Butterfield, now in the act of shaking hands courteously with that pretty little child of the art teacher.

And he watched Martin accept his picture from the hands of the little girl and march with soldierly bearing back to his place.

A manly little chap, after all, the major thought.

Martin resumed his seat with quiet dignity. A moment later the major dismissed the class, thereby causing an exodus not unlike a stampede.

The major did the courtesies with his guests and followed them to the porch.

Outside in the sun, just beyond the guests' parked cars, the art class was reconvened in a milling swirl of shouting and dust.

From the center of the mob, Major Lake and his guests could hear a voice that was fresh in their memories.

"Don't you call me names!" Martin Butterfield was shouting. "You're just sore 'cause you couldn't think up any crazy picture."

"Surrealist! Surrealist! Surrealist!" taunted the voice of Sparky Roberts. There were loud blows, violent epithets and sounds of grunting and groaning.

"Heavens to Betsy!" exclaimed Monsieur Picciotti.

"I knew he was an awful person," said Emily primly.

Major Lake bade his guests good-by and made his way toward the vortex of the whirlpool. It wouldn't be long now until Martin Butterfield's camping period was over and he would be back in his parents' bosom.

Somehow, Major Lake had come to abhor summer as the least of the yearly cycle of seasons.

CHAPTER 7

A Study in Salesmanship

TRAVEL offers a new view of things; it presents new sights and new experiences; it broadens a person. Nobody is more earnestly convinced of the truth of these beliefs than the traveler himself. It matters not at all whether he be fifty or ten, as Martin Butterfield happened to be when he arrived home in Fern Township from Major Lake's summer camp.

When Martin stepped off the train at the township junction and was met by his parents, who tiresomely kissed him in public, there were already certain stirrings in his breast. Martin was bristling with ideas that would demonstrate how much he had been changed by two weeks alone, and away from home, in the broad, big world.

Martin calculated that a good impression made now might get him another trip to summer camp the following year. For Martin was perfectly consistent in his attitude toward camp. He had been reluctant to go; and he had been equally reluctant to leave.

It was no later than suppertime at the Butterfield home when Martin was suddenly inspired to give his mother and father their first glimpse into the beneficial effects of travel on the young mind.

The three of them had gathered around the big table in the dining room, which made it seem like a holiday. It seemed even more like a holiday when Martin discovered a present lying beside his plate, a new and shining Mickey Mouse watch as big as a Christmas ornament.

Martin responded with mute rapture. A watch that went! He said nothing. In utter silence he picked up the timepiece and held it, fob and all, to his ear.

"It ticks!" he said.

"Do you like it, Martin?" his mother inquired.

Martin expressed the inexpressible delight he felt.

"It's all right," he said. "Yep, it's all right."

His mother's eyes shone with pleasure.

Martin's father pulled back his chair with brusque satisfaction. "Well, let's eat, folks," he said happily. "I'm hungrier than four wolves and a wild cat."

Martin wriggled into his chair, still testing his watch.

It was a very fine thing to have a watch, a very grown-up thing.

With his mind lamentably on the wonders of radium dials, Martin said grace, and then his father helped him to the drumstick of a fat brown roasted chicken.

Mr. Butterfield added a scoop of steaming sage dressing and mashed potatoes before he asked a question.

"Well, Martin," he said, "now that you're back home, what are you going to do?"

"I got a good idea," answered Martin with a promptness that awed his father. "I would like to make some money."

"A lot of people have tried that," Mr. Butterfield said. "No reason why you shouldn't."

"I think it's a *very* good idea," Mrs. Butterfield added. "I think it's just fine that you want to *do* things, Martin."

Mr. Butterfield devoted himself blissfully for a moment to the white meat, dark meat, giblets, dressing, potatoes, gravy and peas on his plate.

"Any ideas about *how* you're going to make some money, Martin?" he inquired. "I might be able to use a few tips myself."

"George!" said Mrs. Butterfield warningly.

"I would—for a fact," Mr. Butterfield reiterated.

Martin observed this exchange. He was glad that his father was a doubting Thomas. He, Martin, would now demonstrate that there was one boy around this town who had learned a thing or two.

For Martin's trip to camp had been educational in one respect. During his hours on the train coming home from Major Lake's establishment, he had come by a magazine for boys. In it he had discovered a business that was not only guaranteed to provide a boy with ample pocket money but also with more interesting rewards, such as a blimp, a big blimp. Imagine having your own blimp. . . .

Martin was just imagining it when he was recalled to earth by his father's voice.

"Come on, Martin," Mr. Butterfield was saying, "tell us about it. What kind of business are you going into?"

"I'm going to sell magazines to people," Martin said.

"Magazines?" inquired his father. "What kind of magazines?"

"Any kind," replied Martin. "I'm gonna take sus-critchins."

"Su—which?" Mr. Butterfield asked. "You mean sub-scriptions, don't you?"

"That's what I said," Martin answered stoutly.

"You mean you'll sell them from door to door?" Mrs. Butterfield said, clearly reflecting apprehensions of her son growing up to be a pack peddler.

"Yes, Mother," said Martin impatiently. "I only have to take the orders, that's all."

"Oh," said Mrs. Butterfield.

"Oh-ho!" said Mr. Butterfield.

He mused pleasantly to himself as he carved up a slice of white meat.

"You take orders?" he asked. "And then the people get the magazines and then they get a bill in the mail maybe?"

Martin was agreeably surprised to find that his father was able to understand the whole thing.

"That's it!" he said. "Anybody can see how easy it is. It was all advertised in a magazine I was reading on the train."

He scooped up a large forkful of mashed potatoes and began to eat busily. He was tired of explaining his plans now. Once he got the subscription business going, his mother and father would see what a good thing it was and how much he had learned by traveling on trains.

Mr. Butterfield interrupted this reverie. "Just one more little detail, Martin," he said. "How much do you get out of this and when do you get it?"

Martin was patient with his father.

"I get a quarter for every suscritchin," he replied. "I get it when the people pay for the suscritchin."

He did not feel required to mention the blimp within the strict limits of his father's question. Nor did he feel any impulse to. Perhaps he would not say anything about it until he got it in good working order. Then he would just sail over the house in it; that would surprise everybody.

Martin did not have to wait long for a reply to the coupon he carefully filled out and sent to the magazine publishers. Early in the afternoon exactly two days later, the Fern Township postman deposited in the Butterfield mailbox a large envelope importantly addressed to Mr. Martin Butterfield. Martin was waiting on the porch, as he had been waiting for every mail for two days.

The envelope contained a variety of impressive papers and documents, plus a fascinating little booklet filled with pictures and lists of prizes that were extra to boys who showed ambition, energy, and initiative in selling subscriptions. On the cover of the booklet appeared another picture of the blimp, this time in color and even bigger than it had been before. Martin spent a considerable time contemplating this dazzling object before he studied his instruction sheet.

It was very simple. All people had to do, really, was to sign a card naming the magazine they wished to subscribe to. Then Martin would write his name on the line that boldly said "SALESMAN" and mail it in.

It felt fine to be a "SALESMAN."

Martin decided to embark forthwith upon his selling career. He began instinctively in the true tradition of salesmanship—he attacked the market area he knew.

Having seen peddlers go from door to door along the street on which he lived in Fern Township, Martin decided to follow this orderly pattern in his neighborhood. He began at the house on the corner where the elms cast a peaceful umbrella of shade upon neat lawns and garden borders.

With his envelope under his arm like a brief case, Martin mounted the steps of the front porch, rang the doorbell and waited, rocking on the balls of his feet, as salesmen do when they wait.

When the prospect came to the door, Martin said, "Hello, Mrs. McLaughlin."

The prospect, whose hands were white with flour, said, "Oh, it's only you, Martin."

"Yes," replied Martin. "I came to see if you would like to buy a suscritchin to a magazine."

"A subscription?" said Mrs. McLaughlin, tucking back a wisp of graying hair with her whitened fingers. "Just a moment, Martin, I have some pies in the oven."

Martin whistled softly to himself while he waited for Mrs. McLaughlin to return. It was all so simple that he wondered why he had never gone into business before. All you had to do was get your friends and neighbors . . .

Mrs. McLaughlin returned and studied Martin closely through the doorway.

"Does your mother know about these subscriptions, Martin?" she asked.

"Oh, yes," said Martin. "You see, I just have to take the orders and then . . ."

"Well," Mrs. McLaughlin interrupted, pursing her lips thoughtfully, "we take a lot of magazines that I don't ever seem to get time to read."

Martin rose to the occasion. "I'll bet you don't get all the ones I got to sell," he challenged, shaking out the folder of finely printed lists of publications that Mrs. McLaughlin and her family could enjoy simply by signing one of his cards.

Mrs. McLaughlin glanced over the list and then handed it back to Martin.

"Really, Martin," she said, "I just can't take another magazine around here. We haven't got room for what comes in the mail now."

She paused a moment, sniffing the air.

"My pies!" she cried.

The salesman found himself alone on the porch.

He went down the steps to the street. It was a bitter disappointment. But there were other people who lived on this street who were better friends of his than Mrs. Mc-

Laughlin. Just wait until next Halloween and see who gets their windows soaped—with tallow, too.

Martin arrived on the front porch of the home of Dr. Jonathan Stark, the tall, thin, gaunt, graying physician of Fern Township.

By chance, it was the afternoon that was Dr. Stark's single half holiday in a hard-driving, seven-day physician's week. Also by chance, Dr. Stark was alone at home, in the delightful early moments of an afternoon nap.

Martin twisted the handle of the old-fashioned bell at the entrance.

A moment after the great clang rang out, Martin was suddenly stiffened by the violent opening of the door and the appearance of an angular and angry apparition, which was Dr. Stark peering around the door.

"What in heaven's name do you want, Martin?" roared Dr. Stark in much the same tone he had once used when Martin balked a trifle at being punched with a needle.

Martin stared up at the tousled gray locks of his family's physician, then tried to summon up certain reserves of courage that did not form ranks and march with any willingness.

"Would you like to buy a suscritchin to a magazine, Dr. Stark?" he heard a voice—his own—inquire.

Dr. Stark appeared to undergo a severe attack of some kind of dangerous ailment which caused his eyes to bulge fierily and his Adam's apple to pop up and down vigorously. He stepped from behind the door to reveal the fact that his skinny frame was adorned with no more than BVD's.

He spoke in anguish loud enough to carry into the next block.

"Jumping catfish, a man gets one measly afternoon off and—" He stopped and looked down at Martin in a manner

117

that threatened impending bodily harm. His voice sank to a hoarse whisper. "Wait till I find that father of yours, letting his youngster run around disturbing honest people at this hour of the day," he said illogically.

At this point Martin correctly concluded that Dr. Stark did not wish to buy any magazine subscriptions.

He backed off the porch and half-walked, half-ran down the gravel path to the street with the slam of Dr. Stark's door pounding in his ears.

It was an upsetting experience. Martin's steps toward the next house were less brisk than before; they lagged; presently they ceased altogether and he took a seat on the curb to review his progress.

He held the envelope between his knees but did not open it to read its contents again. Martin felt a faintly stirring desire to abandon the subscription-selling business in favor of some less rigorous enterprise.

Then he thought of the blimp and how he would feel sailing over the Butterfield house at about five o'clock in the afternoon, just at the time his father came home from the office.

The sun was hot overhead and the asphaltic concrete of the street sweated out a heat that rose in waves around the small salesman on the curbstone. He moved to the shade of a neighboring elm and reflected further.

The more he reflected the more certain he became that he had made a fundamental error in his beginning. Instead of attacking a market where he was well known, far wiser would it be to hie himself to the farthest end of the village where he was not among neighbors; the Butterfields' neighbors, it seemed to Martin sitting on the curb, had not behaved very well and he was unwilling to risk himself and his pride on any more of *them*.

Precisely eighteen minutes later, Martin Butterfield began

ringing doorbells at the opposite end of Fern Township, and with precisely the kind of success he had hoped for in the first place. It all happened because Martin alertly discovered a line of salesmanship that worked wonderfully.

It happened quite by accident on the porch of Mrs. Delilah Bussy, a widow lady of very great respectability who occupied a comfortable little house on East Township Road and a far-right soprano seat in the Presbyterian church choir.

Mrs. Bussy, a towering woman, was the delight of small boys at Halloween and their despair when they lost a ball in her yard. Martin found her on the front porch crocheting, an art that was not only useful but also permitted her to observe the comings and goings of her neighbors minutely.

Martin viewed her as a challenge. He needed to prove that he wasn't afraid. With his envelope under his arm and his courage visible for half a block, he sallied up the walk between the fragrant herbaceous borders of Mrs. Bussy's property.

"Good afternoon, Martin," said Mrs. Bussy familiarly before the salesman could speak.

"Good afternoon," Martin replied, echoing her grown-up greeting.

Mrs. Bussy gave him half of her piercing attention, the other half remaining on her flying crochet hook. "What is it, Martin?" she inquired crisply.

Martin was a little unseated by the directness of the customer.

"I came to see you about a suscritchin," he said in an agitated torrent. "Would you like to take a suscritchin to a magazine?"

Mrs. Bussy halted crocheting operations altogether.

"Subscriptions?" she inquired. "Are you selling subscriptions?"

"Yes, ma'am," replied Martin, as if confessing a crime.

Mrs. Bussy's busy little eyes clouded over thoughtfully as she regarded Martin.

"Is your father's business so bad he has to send his little boy out to make money?" she asked.

Martin had not seriously considered this interesting approach to magazine selling before. He was suddenly struck with its possibilities; at the same moment he was struck with a recollection of the first night he got home from camp.

Didn't his father say that *he* could use a few tips about making money? By a process of reasoning that has often been used in human affairs, a process that produces the very thought that the thinker wants, Martin arrived at what he considered a fair statement of the truth.

"Yes," he said soberly to Mrs. Bussy, "I'm trying to help my father by selling magazines."

Mrs. Bussy's eyes glittered at this bit of intelligence, and Martin was gratified to receive not only an expression of her sympathy but an order for a subscription to the lowest-priced magazine on the list.

When he departed from her front porch, his spirits were greatly lifted. He had made his first sale and he had discovered a technique of selling that seemed promising of results.

As the afternoon passed and as Martin progressed from one house to another in the lower end of Fern Township village, there might have been noted a perceptible pick up in the number of telephone calls over the party lines. The voices all repeated the same words.

". . . well, that's a surprise."

". . . you're sure that's what Martin said?"

". . . out of the mouths of babes, you get the truth sometimes."

". . . poor Martha! I always felt that George Butterfield was too good-looking to be much of a success in life."

Meanwhile, and blissfully, Martin went eloquently from
house to house. Never again was the magazine subscription
business to be so good in Fern Township and never in years
had anyone done so much in so short a time to build up
the postman's security in his job of pursuing his appointed
rounds with the U. S. mail.

At supper that night in the Butterfield kitchen, Martin
announced that he had begun his career.

"You mean you've been out working already, Martin?"
Mrs. Butterfield said. "I thought you had gone swimming."

"I haven't got time for swimming now," Martin said
righteously.

Mr. Butterfield grinned good-humoredly at his son.

"How'd it go, boy?" he inquired. "Pretty tough the first
day?"

"I got twenty-seven suscritchins," Martin said modestly.

Before supper was over, Mr. Butterfield privately conceded to himself that Martha had been right about sending
Martin to summer camp. There was no doubt that it had
done something for the boy. Imagine a little kid like that
selling twenty-seven subscriptions in one afternoon!

Meanwhile Martin could scarcely eat his supper, so lost
was he in contemplation of the probability that he would
soon be the owner of a private blimp, not to mention
twenty-seven 25-cent pieces.

The Fern Township post office opened for business only
after the Buckmaster grocery had opened its doors each
morning. It happened that Grocer Buckmaster was also the
postmaster, but private enterprise naturally took precedence
over public affairs.

Martin Butterfield waited impatiently at the little postal

coop in the rear of the grocery while Mr. Buckmaster tedi-
ously opened his big collapsible doors at the front, lowered
his awnings, moved stands of vegetables on to the sidewalk
and cheerfully performed the chores that go with store-
keeping in the early morning. Mr. Buckmaster was bluffly
cheerful.

"You aren't in any big hurry, I hope, Martin," he shouted
as he huffed and puffed in and out of the store carrying his
wares to the outdoors.

"Well . . ." Martin said, "I'd like to get this mailed
pretty quick."

"What have you got there?" Mr. Buckmaster called.
"Some of those magazine orders you sold yesterday?"

"Yes, sir," Martin said.

He was pleased that his work of the previous day had been
sufficient to attract Mr. Buckmaster's favorable attention.

"I heard about it," Mr. Buckmaster said cryptically, "and
I must say I'm surprised you stuck to it like that."

Martin accepted this divided compliment with pleasure.

"It wasn't so hard," he said.

Mr. Buckmaster went behind the postal cage and opened
his window for business.

"Your folks must be pretty proud of you," he said.

This brilliant idea had not occurred to Martin.

"I hope so," he said modestly.

Mr. Buckmaster weighed Martin's envelope. The postage
came to twenty-seven cents even.

Martin fished in his watch pocket for the quarter and
the two pennies but Mr. Buckmaster became suddenly and
inexplicably generous.

"Don't bother about the twenty-seven cents, Martin,"
he said. "You just save that."

Martin was not reluctant to accept this beneficence and

he was equally glad to accept the free candy bar Mr. Buck-master gave him as he left the store.

But he was puzzled about Mr. Buckmaster's parting remark.

"You tell your folks, Martin," said Mr. Buckmaster, "that I'll do anything I can."

"Yes, sir," said Martin, biting into the soft chocolate and caramel of the bar. "I sure will."

As he wandered off up the street, he presently dismissed this odd matter from his mind. No doubt it was one of those meaningless things grown-ups are always saying to each other.

Dawdling along the street, he munched the candy pleas-antly and ruminated on how soon he would be the captain of a blimp flying over Fern Township. These re-flections gave rise to an inevitable result. Martin was pres-ently proceeding up the sidewalk toward his home in a highly erratic fashion and emitting a steady, penetrating buzzing sound. He was, for all practical purposes, already sailing in his blimp—zooming, pausing, climbing and swoop-ing—when Sparky Roberts, his boon friend, loomed up from behind the Roberts hedge.

"What do you think you're doin'?" Sparky inquired abruptly.

Martin halted his airship and grounded himself.

"What's it to you?" he replied. "I wasn't doin' anything much."

"G'wan," Sparky persisted. "What were you doin' there?"

"Nothing," Martin said firmly.

Sparky parted the hedge in a manner that would have tested the patience of his gardening father. He leaped out upon the sidewalk.

"Okay then," he said, "don't tell me."

The two boys stood regarding each other. Martin felt his secret growing larger inside his breast. In a minute, a second—in no time at all—the secret had ballooned to the size of a blimp.

Martin's compartment for secrets was no blimp-hangar.

"Can you keep a secret, Sparky?" he inquired quietly.

"Sure," Sparky said carelessly.

Martin was disappointed. "Okay," he said, "if you don't care I won't tell you."

Sparky was unperturbed.

"I know a secret, too," he said.

Martin emitted what he hoped was a snort of derision.

"You ain't going to get my secret just by making up a secret," he said.

"I didn't make it up," Sparky said defensively. "It's real; it's better'n yours, I bet, and it's about you!"

Martin paused. Maybe Sparky had found out about the blimp.

He adopted a new strategy. "Does it go z-z-z-z-z?" Martin resumed his impersonation of a blimp.

Sparky watched Martin's motions curiously. "What's that?" he asked.

Martin was greatly relieved. He still had a secret to sell.

"Nothing," he said benignly.

The time for dickering had arrived. Both boys settled down on the curb, pushing and elbowing each other.

Sparky made the introductory offer.

"Will you tell me your secret if I tell you mine?"

"Is yours any good?"

"I already told you it's about you, Martin."

Martin thought deeply. "Okay," he said. "You tell yours first."

Sparky plucked a stem of grass from the plot between the curb and the sidewalk.

"Mrs. Bussy told my mother about it," he said. "I heard her."

Martin was impatient. "What did she tell?"

"She says," Sparky said importantly, "that your folks are broke and you have to work."

Martin felt that he had been taken in.

"Is that all the secret you got?" he cried belligerently. "That ain't any secret; it ain't even true."

Sparky's eyes blazed. "Are you going to welsh on your secret?"

"Mrs. Bussy must be crazy," Martin said. "I just saw her yesterday and sold her a suscritchin to a magazine. . . ."

Sparky's eyes lit up. "Is that all the secret you got?" he inquired derisively. "Mrs. Bussy told my mother all about that. I heard her."

It was Martin's turn to scoff. "*That* ain't it," he said. "If you don't look out, Sparky, I won't tell you anything at all."

"Your folks ain't broke then?"

"My folks?" said Martin proudly. "Why, I bet my father makes more money than anybody in this town. He's always got dollar bills in his pocket, just pulls 'em right out when he goes in a store and buys any old thing he wants."

Sparky was visibly impressed.

"What's your secret?" he asked.

"You sure you can keep quiet?"

"Come on," said Sparky threateningly.

"Okay, but don't you tell anybody," Martin said, "and I'll tell you. I'm gonna get a blimp."

In the next minute, Sparky Roberts got himself appointed second officer of Fern Township's only blimp. The next minute after that, the captain of the blimp and his chief subordinate were making their way toward the Butterfield barn to plan for a flight schedule that would make them not only the most envied of all the boys in Fern Township but the wealthiest as well.

While the Butterfield barn was buzzing and murmuring with pleasant ideas about blimps, another and speedier tableau was unfolding in the Butterfield house.

It began just at nine o'clock when Mrs. Butterfield answered the telephone and found Mrs. Roberts, mother of Sparky, on the line.

Mrs. Butterfield settled down in the chair beside the phone for a good, long, friendly tête-a-tête.

"Oh, Connie," she said into the mouthpiece, "I was just going to give you a ring."

Mrs. Roberts' voice came back clearly so that there was no question about the remarkable words she used.

"You can count on us if there's anything we can do, Martha," she said. "Sam heard all about it at the office and we agreed we would do anything . . ."

Mrs. Butterfield was intrigued with this statement.

"Heard all about what?" she said. "Am I missing something, Connie?"

There was a definite break in Mrs. Roberts' voice even over the telephone. "Brave girl!" she said.

Mrs. Butterfield was puzzled but not nearly so puzzled then as she became a moment later when Mrs. Roberts hung up, saying she would be right over.

Martin Butterfield's mother sat in the chair with an odd feeling. Then she suffered a sharp catch in her throat.

Could there be something wrong with Martin? She half rose from the chair before she recalled she had just seen him pass the window on his way to the barn.

George? Had George been struck by a car downtown? She was just reaching for the receiver when the phone began to ring.

She clapped it to her ear in time to hear her husband's voice inquire:

"What are you doing, Martha? Sitting right on the phone?"

"Oh, George!" Mrs. Butterfield cried. "You're all right then?"

"All right?" he said irritably. "I guess so. Shouldn't I be?"

Mrs. Butterfield paused.

"Well," she said, "Connie Roberts just called up here and it was the oddest thing—she offered to do all she could for us!"

There was a brief silence on the other end of the line. Mrs. Butterfield could hear the secretary's typewriter ticking in Mr. Butterfield's law office.

"That's funny," Mr. Butterfield said at last. "I just had a call from Sam Roberts and he offered me as much money as I needed. No sooner had he hung up than Buck Buckmaster came booming in here to tell me I could have as much credit as I want. What's it all about, anyway, Martha?"

Mrs. Butterfield said, "I just can't imagine, George."

She sat holding the phone to her ear, eyeing the toe of her pump, which she turned in a slow little circle.

Her husband spoke again. "I feel like the victim of a great tragedy, except that I don't know what the tragedy is."

"Connie Roberts is coming over right away," Mrs. Butterfield said.

"What's she—" Mr. Butterfield began. Then he paused and there was a silence at the other end of the phone. Mrs. Butterfield could almost hear her husband's processes of reasoning working inside his head and she was perfectly

prepared for the question when it came, loud and belligerent, over the telephone line of the Fern Township Telephone Company Limited.

"Where's Martin?" Mr. Butterfield shouted. "When we
get to the bottom of this, I am absolutely certain that we
will uncover your son."

"You always say 'your son' when Martin gets into trouble," Mrs. Butterfield said with some pique.

"In any case," continued Mr. Butterfield, "I'm coming
right over. You find Martin, Martha, before these people
get me to feeling so sorry for myself I'll be taking their
charity."

Mr. Butterfield hung up before Mrs. Butterfield could
reply. As she rose, she heard the steps of Mrs. Roberts on
the front porch.

Mrs. Roberts did not bother to ring. She entered.

"Oh, Martha," she suddenly wailed as she burst into the
room, "why didn't you tell me?"

Mrs. Butterfield did not have an opportunity to reply
before the doorbell rang.

Through the window she observed the bulk of Mrs.
Delilah Bussy. Mrs. Bussy was carrying a basket neatly
covered with a napkin. On the walk behind her loomed
the form of Mr. Butterfield, who had apparently come
home from the office on the dead run.

Mrs. Butterfield saw her husband speak sharply to Mrs.
Bussy and she could hear the sound of his voice but not
the words. She only observed that Mrs. Bussy registered a
look of surprise and shock before she bundled up her basket and departed the Butterfield property in considerable
haste.

When he burst in the front doorway, Mr. Butterfield
had only one question:

"Well," he said, "where's Martin?"

Ideas and discussions, if they are any good, inevitably must be followed by action. After Martin and Sparky had exhausted their entire store of ideas as regarded blimps, balloons, and dirigibles, they bethought themselves of a preparation that could be made immediately for their aërial operations.

When Martin heard his mother's voice calling him to the house, he was behind the dog kennels, busily filling burlap bags with earth for use as ballast on his blimp.

Martin went reluctantly, while Sparky Roberts continued the work.

As he climbed the back porch steps, Martin recognized the first storm signal. His mother was waiting for him with a steadily tapping foot.

The blimp captain said, "What do you want, Mom?"

"Your father wants to speak to you, Martin," his mother replied.

Martin marched silently into the house. A hasty scouring of his memory left him with a clear conscience, although he could never be quite sure when the world around him was going to change the rules and thus catch him off base.

In the living room, Martin found his father talking with Mrs. Roberts.

"Of course it's all a lot of nonsense, Connie," Mr. Butterfield was saying. "It was spread all over town by that old battleax, Mrs. Bussy—oh, here you are, Martin!"

Martin stopped in the middle of the room. "Hello, Dad," he said quietly.

Mr. Butterfield rubbed his hands in a way that always worried witnesses in court. Meanwhile he looked steadily at his son.

"Martin," he said, "how many magazine subscriptions did you sell yesterday?"

Martin replied, "Twenty-seven."

"Martin," said his father, "did you tell people that we were out of money and you had to go to work?"

Mrs. Butterfield cleared her throat. She couldn't stand this.

"Connie," she said suddenly to Mrs. Roberts, "why don't you come out in the kitchen and have a cup of coffee?"

Before Mrs. Roberts reached the door, however, Martin emitted the frightful truth.

"I didn't tell them that, Dad," he said. "I only told 'em I was helping you. You said you could use some tips on how to make money."

It was a beautifully aimed shaft and, if it did not strike a target in his father, it struck one in the softer metal of his mother.

With a mother's instinct, she took the part of her off-spring—nay, she seized it triumphantly.

"Why, George," she said, "those were your very words."

Mr. Butterfield looked like a general who discovers his troops are facing five enemy armies instead of the one he had been told to expect.

He coughed, flushed deeply and fished in his jacket for his pipe.

"Martin," he said, "I hope you made enough money to make it worth your trouble."

It was a good moment for Martin to reveal his secret. It might cheer his father up and it might improve Martin's chances for surviving the day without punishment.

"The money isn't anything, Dad," he said. "I'm gonna get a blimp."

Mr. Butterfield paused in his pipe loading and stared for a moment.

"A blimp," he said, "is just what we need."

Martin shifted from one foot to the other. "Well," he said

finally, "I got to get back out there and get to work. Sparky and I have to get ready for the blimp. When it comes, we'll make a lot of money giving people rides."

Martin smiled sweetly at his mother as he passed from the room.

The blimp arrived in the mail two days later. It came in a large flat package. It was quite a lot smaller than the picture had made it seem. And it was not exactly the same shape, because you had to put it together yourself out of a mass of sticks and paper and glue.

Martin was deeply disappointed.

However, his disappointment was assuaged by the present of a new air rifle which was purchased by his father at the Fern Township Hardware and Iron Store.

Martin was surprised to receive such a substantial present for no reason at all. It was neither his birthday nor Christmas.

And his father did not explain the gift.

When Mr. Butterfield brought the gun home, he just handed it to Martin and turned to Mrs. Butterfield.

"Maybe this will remove the possibility of child labor for a while," he said.

That evening Martin and Sparky Roberts removed two windows from the barn and brought down a total of three sparrows.

"Things are getting back to normal around here," Mr. Butterfield observed to his wife as the second window tinkled in the back yard.

CHAPTER 8

Uncle Jonathan

SUMMER in Fern Township was like summer wherever small boys live. At any given moment of the day, Martin Butterfield might find time hanging heavy on his hands. There were idle afternoons spent lying on the old auto seat in the barn; there were long mornings devoted to mowing the lawn, under orders from his father; there were smoky, warm evenings passed with Sparky Roberts, Red Spingarn, Stinker Larrabee, and others on the back fence where the soft evening air murmured with the old story of What I'm Going to Do When I Grow Up.

At each of these moments time seemed to move slowly; it seemed to be in inexhaustible supply. Summer was a permanent season.

And yet a funny thing happened. Before Martin Butterfield realized what had occurred, it was the middle of August. School was only two weeks away.

This fact loomed like an ever-growing cloud on the horizon of his mind.

He was forcibly reminded of the impending beginning

of lessons one day at lunch by his father. Martin spent at
least half an hour lying on the old auto seat in the barn that
afternoon—just thinking. Having calculated that two weeks
added up to fourteen days, and fourteen days added up to
quite a lot of freedom yet remaining to him, he arose briskly
from his dusty couch and prepared to leave the back yard
for Sparky Roberts' house and whatever distant points
might occur to two active minds.

The execution of Martin's vague summer afternoon plan
had progressed as far as the back gate when his mother's
voice came clearly through the kitchen window.

"Martin!" she called. "I've been looking for you. Where
have you been?"

"Around," said Martin with that geographical exactness
which sons habitually use on inquisitive parents.

He hung on the gate for a moment, awaiting the inevitable; the inevitable occurred.

"Will you come in here, please, Martin?" his mother said.
"Hurry now."

Martin hurried slowly, with visions of onerous tasks such
as going to the store, taking a bath, or otherwise flagrantly
wasting a precious afternoon.

When he entered the sunny kitchen, he found his mother
looking at a telegram.

Martin's spirits livened. Telegrams meant excitement.

"What's happened?" he inquired.

His mother looked at him with preoccupation.

"Your Great-uncle Jonathan is coming," she said, continuing to look at the telegram. "I must call your father right
away and tell him." She started suddenly for the living
room, that distant look still in her eye.

"Uncle Jonathan!" cried Martin. "Wow . . ."

His voice trailed ecstatically.

He heard his mother's voice speaking into the telephone:

"Yes, George, this very afternoon; he's coming on the four o'clock train. Why, certainly, you'll have to go with us. I thought this might be one year when it wouldn't be our turn for a visit . . ."

Martin wasted no more time listening to his mother's low conversation on the telephone. Instead, and with unwonted swiftness, he climbed the stairs two at a time and headed for the bathroom where he willingly and voluntarily —without duress of any kind—ran hot water into the tub, undressed and prepared to take a bath.

Uncle Jonathan! If Uncle Jonathan were slightly less than eagerly welcomed by the grown-ups among the relatives he chose to visit, it could be stated with equal truth that he was highly popular among the smaller fry.

Uncle Jonathan was a very old man. But he was a very brisk and active gentleman. He seemed to know exactly what children like to do and what they do not like to do. Furthermore, he had a pocket that was literally flowing with small coins which were spent in the most enchanting ways in candy stores, ice-cream stores, hardware stores, grocery stores, motion-picture theaters, and other institutions that give a person a real return for his money.

Martin was in the bath tub busily scrubbing himself before his mother came upstairs.

"Are you in the tub, Martin?" Mrs. Butterfield asked.

"Yes, ma'am," said Martin courteously. You'd think a person never took a bath around here.

He was all dressed in his Sunday clothes, his face shining and his dark hair brushed to a shimmering glaze an hour before train time. Mrs. Butterfield peered at her son with an air of foreboding.

On the first morning of Uncle Jonathan's visit, a lavish breakfast was prepared at the Butterfield home. Disappointingly, however, the guest did not put in an appearance for waffles, ham, decorated grapefruit, and other delicacies.

"Where do you suppose he could have taken Martin at this hour?" Mrs. Butterfield asked her husband.

Mr. Butterfield drummed his fingers on the table. "How long is he going to stay—that's the question!" he retorted.

Mrs. Butterfield waited until 8:00 A.M. and then served a forlorn meal to her husband and herself in a setting of pristine linen and glittering silver.

The meal was half-finished when Uncle Jonathan and his admiring grandnephew were to be heard coming up the street.

For a man of his advanced years, Uncle Jonathan retained a voice as remarkable for its depth as for its carrying power. Uncle Jonathan had been a basso in the church choir of his town for more than half a century and when he felt like singing, he sang.

Faintly at first, through the Butterfield windows, came the singing voice of Uncle Jonathan, then more clearly, finally with such painful clarity that Mr. Butterfield laid down his fork and observed to his wife:

"Our neighbors must be enjoying this."

"Now, George," Mrs. Butterfield said patiently, "Uncle Jonathan means well."

"Even when he sings?" Mr. Butterfield asked.

His remark was barely audible, due to the strains of a song familiar enough in some parts of the world, although hardly a morning hymn to the sun in Fern Township:

> *"She was a fishmonger*
> *And that was no wonder*
> *For so were her father and mother before;*
> *Through streets broad and narrow*
> *She wheeled her wheelbarrow,*
> *Crying, 'Cockles and mussels—alive, alive, OH!' "*

The last syllable was pronounced on the front porch from which point Mr. and Mrs. Butterfield heard Uncle Jonathan say, "Maybe we better quiet down, Martin. Your folks, like as not, are still in bed."

Mrs. Butterfield arose from the table with a quick, admonishing glance at her husband and went to the door to meet her uncle and son. The trio entered the dining room in an aura of noisy good fellowship, Mrs. Butterfield leading the old man and the boy.

Mr. Butterfield rose to shake hands with his uncle-in-law.

"Good morning, sir," he said with an admirable show of tolerance.

"Morning, George," said Uncle Jonathan. "Didn't know lawyers got up before noon."

Uncle Jonathan sat down at the table, while Martin wriggled reluctantly into a chair opposite him.

Uncle Jonathan was a big man, slightly stooped with years. He had a remarkable lot of gray wiry hair that seemed to be unacquainted with a comb. His face was wrinkled around the eyes and mouth, but it was an unworried, untroubled face, deeply tanned. His eyes were a blue that was deepened through the lenses of his spectacles.

Mrs. Butterfield moved to the waffle iron beside her place and prepared to pour a pitcher of golden batter over the sizzling grids.

"You're just in time for breakfast, Uncle Jonathan," she said gaily.

Uncle Jonathan held up a halting hand.

"Don't make any for us," he ordered. "We just *had* breakfast."

Mrs. Butterfield looked at her uncle and then at Martin questioningly.

"You ate already?" she asked. "Why, none of the restaurants in town are open yet."

Uncle Jonathan chuckled deeply and then winked at Martin.

"That's all she knows about this old town," he said. "We had breakfast down in Mike's All Night Shack on the state highway."

Martin nodded with satisfaction. "I had four hamburgers," he said, "with pickles, onion, ketchup and relish. I'm not very hungry, I guess," he added thoughtfully.

Mr. Butterfield looked at Mrs. Butterfield but he did not say anything. Mr. Butterfield was a patient man with an essentially amiable view of the fellow members of his race.

Martin felt fine.

The morning thus far had been remarkable for Martin Butterfield. It was the first time in his recollection that anybody had ever let him, freely and fully, test his capacity for hamburgers. Now, in retrospect, he was a trifle disappointed with the result; after the third one, hamburgers lost some of their delectable glamour. Just knowing that there were an unlimited number of hamburgers in the bush reduced the succulent pleasures of the hamburger in the hand.

His diminished pleasure did not, however, affect his enthusiasm for a great-uncle who was willing to haul off and make such a scientific test possible.

He looked across the table at Uncle Jonathan who was now absent-mindedly poking a fork at and otherwise destroying a half grapefruit garnished with maraschino cherries.

"Yes, sir," said Uncle Jonathan, "we've had a fine morning, me and Martin, and there's still a whole day to go."

Martin was overwhelmed with the prospect.

"How long are you gonna visit us, Uncle Jonathan?" he asked, thereby expressing a question in some other minds.

"Are you anxious for me to go home right away, Martin?" retorted his uncle.

"I'll say not!" Martin said truthfully.

Uncle Jonathan laughed. "I'll be around awhile, Martin," he said happily. "Don't you worry—or you either, George!"

"I won't," said Mr. Butterfield.

After Mr. Butterfield left the house for the office and Mrs. Butterfield began work on the breakfast dishes, the early-rising visitor went upstairs for his mid-morning nap.

It seemed an odd time, in Martin's opinion, to take a nap, but he was willing to excuse Uncle Jonathan in the light of his other virtues. Martin repaired to the rear of the Butterfield yard and the beagle kennels.

He drew a box up to the wire along the dog pen and poked his finger through the wire, letting the old beagle mother lick and nuzzle his hand while her growing babies surged around her in an upheaval of brown ears and black and white spots.

"Good old Gypsy," Martin murmured benevolently, and he scratched her behind her flop-ears contentedly. Spreading his benison still wider, he scratched the pups' ears in turn.

He wondered how long Uncle Jonathan would sleep; it was certainly a strange and wasteful thing to do on a summer morning when the world was beckoning, a world full of woods and rivers and dogs and singing birds and five-and-dime stores and ice-cream parlors.

Martin felt that an ice-cream cone would go very well right now. It would kind of offset . . .

His thought was interrupted by a pair of hands swiftly covering his eyes and by Sparky Roberts' voice shouting: "Who is it? I won't let ya go till ya tell who it is!"

"Cut that out," Martin ordered and he wriggled briskly out of Sparky's grasp, rubbing his brow. "You want to blind somebody?"

Sparky calmly took a seat beside him.

"What you doin'?" he asked.

Martin was still not fully assuaged. "Nothin'," he replied.

The two boys sat in silence.

"Where's your Uncle Jonathan?" asked Sparky. "Didn't he come?"

"Sure, he came," said Martin. "Where he is, is for me to know and you to find out."

Sparky shoved. Martin shoved back. In a moment, by the inevitable laws of nature, the two friends were locked in combat and rolling about on the ground in the golden morning sun.

How long they would have been engaged is an open question. The war was brought to truce by the introduction of the toe of an old-fashioned button-up shoe inserted from directly overhead.

"Punkest fight I ever saw in my life," said Uncle Jonathan.

Martin and Sparky disengaged with enough speed to discount both their expressions of reluctance to quit the combat.

"We were just playing," Martin apologized.

"Fooling like," said Sparky.

"Oh," said Uncle Jonathan. "In that case you wouldn't be interested in going for a walk, I guess. Too busy playing."

"I like walking," Martin said stoutly.

"Me, too," Sparky said. "I like a good old walk."

Uncle Jonathan tugged at the rim of his old yellowed Panama hat. He looked at both boys and then he looked speculatively at the kennel in which the old mother dog and her growing offspring were standing up, paws against the wire, grinning, dog-laughing and squeakily whining for neighborliness. At the same instant, Martin and his great-uncle had an identical thought, the kind of gentle thought that is purely reasonable to the minds of old men and small boys, if to nobody else.

"How about the dogs?" asked Martin, who was fully aware of the fact that his father had certain rules about the beagles.

"A dog or two adds a lot to a morning walk," Uncle Jonathan said thoughtfully.

"Nothing like a dog," Sparky said, adding his mite to the snowballing sentiment for freeing imprisoned canines.

"I guess it would be pretty nice for the dogs," said Uncle Jonathan considerately. "We ought to think of them."

He opened the gate, and the old she-dog with her pups tumbled out into the open with joyful little streakings about the legs of the hiking party.

Uncle Jonathan led the way out the back gate.

The party headed down the traditional routes of youth —by back lanes and alleys—through Fern Township village to Lick Creek bridge. They paused in the center of the shining silver span to spit solemnly into the creek and see how far down it was to the water; then they left the main highway, cutting across the lush August pastures toward the wooded hills near the town.

The pups flopped clumsily in the deep grass, following their busy maternal parent who pressed her cold wet nose to the ground, now here and now there, as she reconstructed in her mind the animal traffic that had passed that way during the morning hours before her arrival. The pups emulated her, and Martin Butterfield took proud satisfaction in this exhibition.

"Them puppies are gonna be good rabbit dogs," Martin said. "My daddy knows how to train good rabbit dogs."

Uncle Jonathan tramped along quietly for a moment, with the hurt air of a man who has been challenged.

"He don't know no more about dogs than I do, I bet," he said.

Martin was surprised and a little aggrieved by this reply.

It seemed a slur on the good name of his own father; yet, Uncle Jonathan was "company" and one had to be polite.

Moreover, Martin did not want to make Uncle Jonathan mad for reasons aside from his status as a guest—there was always the ice-cream store to be considered.

"Well, my father knows quite a lot," he said in an attempt at compromise.

Help and aid came suddenly to Uncle Jonathan—from Sparky Roberts, who also was thinking of the ice-cream store.

"I'll bet your Uncle Jonathan is the best," he announced bluntly.

Uncle Jonathan waxed modest. He looked at the dogs racing back and forth ahead of him in the pasture and studied them with a grave air.

"I wouldn't go so far as to say that," he said.

Martin, walking beside his uncle, felt much relieved. He could not—and would not—be traitorous to his father; at the same time, he did not want to do or say anything that might make Uncle Jonathan go home before a proper number of nickels and dimes had blessed various merchants of Fern Township.

But Martin's feeling of relief was to be short-lived.

Uncle Jonathan might feel modest about his accomplishments as a dog handler, but he obviously had no intention of letting his modesty prevent him from demonstrating that he was a man with a way with a dog.

"There's no use just talking. The best thing to do is to show who knows what," said Uncle Jonathan. "We'll go up in the woods and put the dogs to work."

He waved toward the green wooded hills above the pasture.

"Now we're gonna see something real," said Sparky Roberts with perfect allegiance to Uncle Jonathan.

Martin glared at Sparky. Who did he think he was? What was he trying to do, anyway—steal somebody's uncle?

Martin silently gave Sparky an unobtrusive but solid poke with his elbow. "Mind your own business," he said, as Uncle Jonathan strode off to whistle up the dogs and round them up for the exhibition.

"I *am* mindin' my own business," Sparky retorted, "and you better watch out who you push with your elbow."

"They're my dogs," Martin said.

"They're your father's dogs, 'cause I know 'cause he was the only one who was allowed to give me one that time when you climbed on the bridge," Sparky declared.

"Just the same, when he's not here they're the same as my dogs and I get the say about them," Martin said.

Sparky indicated Uncle Jonathan busily rounding up the pack of playful beagles and coming toward them.

"Looks like your uncle don't know it," he said. "Looks like your uncle can do anything with 'em he wants to do."

"My father can do anything, too," said Martin.

"You better be careful what you say to your uncle, Martin," Sparky said in a tone of friendly advice. "He might go home the first thing you know and then we wouldn't . . ."

"You're just hanging around to get free ice cream," Martin whispered bitterly.

"I ain't neither," said Sparky nobly. "I like Uncle Jonathan."

"He's not your uncle and don't you dare call him that . . ." threatened Martin.

The yelping dogs closed around them and mercifully drowned out the argument about proprietary rights to uncles.

"Come on, men," Uncle Jonathan said briskly. "We'll just go up in that patch of woods and see how's about a rabbit. Nothing prettier than hearing a beagle run a rabbit. Just like an outdoor pipe organ, I always claim."

"Better," said Sparky stoutly.

"My father shot thirty-seven rabbits last hunting season," Martin volunteered quietly.

"Brush gun or rifle?" asked Uncle Jonathan.

"He didn't use either one," said Martin knowledgeably. "He used a twelve-gauge shotgun."

"Humph," said Uncle Jonathan, "that's a brush gun."

"Anybody knows a twelve-gauge is a brush gun," said Sparky, who had just been apprised of that fact for the first time in his life.

Martin began to weary very heavily of Sparky Roberts. "Your father hasn't even got a two-gauge shotgun," he said.

"Who ever heard of a two-gauge shotgun?" Sparky retorted.

Uncle Jonathan maneuvered his lanky form so that he fell into stride between the two boys just at the critical moment.

"Tut, tut," he tutted. "Let us not have any odious and invidious comparisons of fathers."

"Any what?" asked Martin.

"No more fightin'," said Uncle Jonathan briefly.

The trio marched up the hill after the dogs. The old she-dog seemed to sense, as they followed her, that something was now expected of her. To her canine mind a woodland, with fences along its edges and brush piles and rock heaps in its midst, meant only one thing—running furry beasts. She began to go about her business, head down, tail up, with darting little dashes and retracings. Behind the old dog, the puppies fell into similar detective attitudes, in the ancient instinct of their kind.

It was a pretty sight, six black and white and brown spots of movement sweeping up the hillside toward the woods on the bright green carpet of summer, six tails whipping whitely in the sun and the sound of heavy, excited sniffing on the air.

"Ever see any dogs work better than that for *anybody?*" inquired Uncle Jonathan.

Martin hesitated. That was the way beagles always worked, even puppies, if they were any good.

Sparky Roberts said, "You sure know your stuff, Uncle Jonathan."

Where did he come off calling Uncle Jonathan uncle?

"Heck," Martin said, "that's 'cause they're beagles. That's the way beagles do." He showed how beagles do by leaping about in the grass and going *sniff-sniff-sniff*.

Uncle Jonathan smiled patiently, but Sparky Roberts was reproachful.

"You should have more respect for your uncle, Martin," he said, feeling an onslaught of good manners.

"I'll give you a good poke on the nose," Martin said.

"You do and—"

"Cease fire, men," said Uncle Jonathan. "The dogs have picked up something."

Sure enough, just above them where the dark fringe of the woodland cast its silent shadow, the old beagle was acting like a kitten that had found the mysterious loose end of a string.

She lashed back and forth for a moment, her ears flapping in frenzy. Her children clumsily lashed back and forth with her, but without her veteran sense of purpose.

Then, while Martin and his Uncle Jonathan and Sparky watched, she suddenly yipped a good, loud, clear yip, calling her brood to attention.

"She's got something already," Uncle Jonathan observed. "All you have to do with a dog is know enough to take her where there's something to find."

This sounded vaguely to Martin like another thrust at his father.

"My father always gets as many rabbits as anybody else," he said defensively.

But Uncle Jonathan was not listening now. He was standing still with his hands on his hips, watching the dogs race off on a definite scent, the mother baying the full, deep cry of the beagle and the pups yipping hopefully.

The dogs disappeared into the woods and Sparky and Uncle Jonathan moved after them.

Martin watched Uncle Jonathan and Sparky with mild surprise as they followed the chase. You don't have to follow a beagle, he thought slowly; a beagle will bring the rabbit back in a circle.

It occurred to him that his Uncle Jonathan was ignorant of this simple fact known to any beagle. It did not, of course, surprise him that a dumb-bell such as Sparky Roberts would be ignorant of almost everything worth-while.

Martin ran after his fellow hunters.

"Hey," he puffed, "why don't we stay right here? She'll bring the rabbit back around."

"Don't want to miss the fun," Uncle Jonathan said, pausing abruptly to remove his hat and wipe his brow for a moment. Then he reconsidered; apparently the fun did not outweigh the effort necessary.

"Let's pick a shady spot and sit down," he suggested.

In the woods above, the old dog's voice was clear and strong. The pups could not be heard now; they hadn't yet learned baying, among other things.

"A rabbit always runs in a circle," Martin explained.

He wanted it to be clear to his great-uncle that he was only trying to be helpful; he didn't want to argue.

"I'll bet they don't sometimes—*some* rabbits, that is," offered Sparky.

Martin momentarily lost his patience and his attitude of amelioration. "Oh, shut up, Sparky," he said.

"We'll see," said Uncle Jonathan gently. He was still perspiring from his uphill climb and he seemed to be suffering some doubts about the wisdom of his active demonstration with beagles.

The dog's voice rose and fell, rose and fell, as it pursued its quarry up over a ridge, first on the near side and then on the far side,

"She's sure got him on the run," said Martin.

"I wonder how the pups are doing," said Sparky.

As if in answer, and very close, there was a sudden loud yipping in the woods—first one voice and then a whole kennelful of voices.

Uncle Jonathan started. "By golly, the puppies got something, too," he said, as if this fact vindicated him. "By George!"

"You just put 'em right where they could find something," said Sparky Roberts.

Uncle Jonathan rose to his feet and started off, Martin and Sparky following. "We'll just go up and see what those pups are accomplishing," he said.

The trio moved into the shaded depths of the wood, and before they had gone a hundred feet they uniformly suffered a visible doubt. Ten feet farther, all doubt was removed. Beside a large fallen log circled five beagle puppies in the process of education related to matters of forest, field, and stream.

On their first hunting attempt in the great wide world of Fern Township, the beagle puppies of Attorney Butterfield had caught a large skunk which was vigorously and fragrantly capable of defending itself.

Its defense hung, at the moment, like heavy smoke on the forested hillside and the pups, standing in a circle, their

146

tails drooping, gave varying evidences of declining enthusiasm for the hunt.

"A skunk!" Martin muttered hoarsely. "Look out!"

He backed away to a respectable range and was gratified that his uncle and Sparky followed suit so that he, Martin, could not be accused of cowardice.

The hunters' appearance on the scene was the excuse for breaking off the engagement that the pups had been waiting for.

With great leaping bounds, the five dogs made for their friends.

Martin held his nose while he picked up a stick and threatened the leading dog. Uncle Jonathan clucked his tongue in his teeth and headed back down the hill.

Sparky looked on in awe and wonder—but only for a moment.

"Wait till your father smells those dogs, Martin," he said with a sobriety not unmixed with speculative anticipation. Then Sparky fled.

Martin devoted his attention busily to the dogs.

"Get away, you . . ." he yelled. "Get away!"

He waved his arms wildly and kicked with one foot, then the other.

The puppies, surprised and then aggrieved, thus learned their second lesson of the day, a brief study of the fickleness of human beings. They backed off and then stole away through the woods, making their separate ways toward their home kennel in Mr. Butterfield's back yard.

Martin, meanwhile, made *his* lonely way to the edge of the woods where he saw his uncle sitting in the grass, looking out over the summer afternoon view of Fern Township.

Uncle Jonathan, far from sharing Martin's concern, seemed as placid as the quiet country scene that lay below them.

147

As Martin emerged from the trees, Sparky Roberts climbed the fence into the pasture at a more distant point.

When the two boys had rejoined him, Uncle Jonathan looked from one to the other benignly. Far away, the old dog's voice could be heard for a moment.

"She sure is a busy dog," the old man said happily.

His manner was sublimely optimistic, as if no canine had ever met a skunk more than socially.

The boys sat down.

"Did you see the puppies come out of the woods yet, Uncle Jonathan?" Martin inquired.

"No, I didn't," answered Uncle Jonathan. "I guess they went home." He chuckled, as if it were actually funny. "That's what I always do if a skunk gets me," he added. "I always go home."

Sparky said, "I guess they learned something that time."

"Education," declared Uncle Jonathan, "is a great thing. Everybody learns something from this—even an old fellow like myself."

That an old man might be expected to learn something was a startling concept to Martin. "What?" he asked bluntly.

"Why," said Uncle Jonathan, "I guess I'll learn how to decontaminate a beagle, because you and me, Martin, are going to be washing up a few dogs as soon as your daddy gets home from work today."

There is always something miraculous about an optimist. Uncle Jonathan was an optimist. Listening to him, Martin suddenly was less concerned about his immediate future at home. Everything would be all right.

Sparky Roberts spoke up. "Can I help decontammelate or whatever it is you're gonna do, Uncle Jonathan?" he asked.

Uncle Jonathan looked down at Sparky sternly. "I don't know," he said. "You think you could learn?"

148

"I can do anything Martin can do," said Sparky.

Martin's wandering thoughts came into sudden, sharp focus.

"You talk so big," he began. "You always . . ."

"Tut, tut," said Uncle Jonathan. "Fighting on such a peaceful day." He waved his arm toward the town lying below them far away. "This is the kind of day when everybody should feel good."

The two boys subsided, each making a bold attempt to feel good toward everybody, with one appropriate exception.

Uncle Jonathan said, "You know what would make *me* feel good? Some ice cream!"

He climbed stiffly to his feet, jingled some coins in his pocket, and looked around at his audience.

"How would that go?" he inquired.

Martin Butterfield and Sparky Roberts agreed that it would go pretty good right now.

The old man and the two boys set off toward the town.

Walking down the hill, Martin stayed close to his great-uncle. The best part of having Uncle Jonathan for a visitor was that you could do so many wonderful things, and meanwhile the natural laws of the universe were suspended.

CHAPTER 9

Fire!

As UNCLE Jonathan said to Mr. Butterfield that evening, there's one thing about a puppy that gets mixed up with a skunk: he isn't very hard to locate.

That was the only good thing anybody could find to say. Mr. Butterfield was obviously displeased with Martin that evening, and Martin wasn't so sure but what his father was pretty mad at Uncle Jonathan too. Martin was more perturbed about the latter than the former. He had survived many a crisis, whereas Uncle Jonathan . . .

But Mrs. Butterfield showed kind concern for Uncle Jonathan.

"It could have happened to anybody," she said.

"Funny it never happened to me in twenty years of hunting," observed Mr. Butterfield.

That was queer, Martin thought. "You're pretty lucky, Dad," he said.

As he went up the stairs, Martin noted, through the banisters looking down over the living room, that his mother and Uncle Jonathan were putting up the card table to play double solitaire, while Mr. Butterfield sat in the large wing chair, reading the paper and, from time to time, raising his nose and testing the evening air.

Martin watched for a moment and then proceeded thoughtfully to his room.

He hoped that his father would do nothing to cause Uncle Jonathan to depart. He slept on that hope. And sleeping did wonders for his troubles. He awoke to a rainy day, a dull gray day, but his spirits were as bright as a Mazda bulb.

With a wonderful humility, Martin resolved to spend this day in being good and useful and worthy, to make up for certain deficits he felt he had incurred yesterday in his father's estimate of filial conduct. Furthermore, and with a generosity that was all-encompassing, Martin Butterfield would help his great-uncle Jonathan to behave in a manner that would improve *his* situation in the household.

The first good thing that Martin would do was simple: he would keep his great-uncle away from the dog kennels. Further plans were a little vague in Martin's mind, but the day was young. He would think of more things to do as situations arose, he was sure.

As is often the case, a situation arose immediately and Martin took full advantage of it.

It was only 6:15 A.M. when Martin quietly tiptoed down the stairs. His parents were not up yet he was quite sure. The sound of movement that he heard on the lower story of the Butterfield house could come only from the Butterfields' fascinating relative.

Sure enough, Uncle Jonathan was in the kitchen, looking out the rain-splashed window impatiently while a percolator of coffee sang the initial notes of its boiling song on the gas range.

Uncle Jonathan turned and looked at his great-nephew, who had considerately not made any noise upstairs by activities along the line of washing, combing or tooth brushing.

"Morning, Martin," said Uncle Jonathan. "Some rain, isn't it?"

Martin looked out the window.

"Good and hard," he replied.

"It ruins a whole morning when it rains so early," Uncle Jonathan declared.

"Yeah," mused Martin. "It sure does."

"But it will kind of lay the smell around the dog pens," Uncle Jonathan speculated.

"Yes, *sir*," said Martin. "A good clean rain will wash off a dog."

The pot on the stove began to bubble with steamy vigor.

"You allowed to have coffee, Martin?" his uncle asked.

"I don't know," Martin said, straining the truth slightly.

Uncle Jonathan poured his own cup and then poured a second.

"Won't hurt you," he said. "I been drinking coffee since I was four. Some day some expert is going to find out coffee is good for kids. They give babies bananas and hard-boiled eggs nowadays. Used to think such stuff would kill 'em."

Martin and his great-uncle sat down to toast and coffee and Martin felt very grown-up.

Uncle Jonathan dunked his toast. "I guess we didn't do so good yesterday, did we, Martin?" he said.

"No, I don't guess we did," Martin said, agreeing with this remarkable understatement.

"You know how to fix a thing like that up, Martin?" asked Uncle Jonathan.

Martin, who had much previous experience in attempting to "fix" things, confessed that it was sometimes a problem.

Uncle Jonathan munched his toast and looked out at the rain contemplatively.

"I'll tell you what to do when you get in a kind of mess, Martin," he said. "The first thing to do is: don't get mad at the people you're in a mess with."

He beamed on his great-nephew generously. "You just kind of overlook the way people act," he continued, "and then you do something nice to make up for the mess."

This seemed a perfectly logical solution to Martin: it lay along the very lines of his own thinking.

"We could do something nice for Dad," Martin said, bringing the matter suddenly down to cases.

His great-uncle smiled and buttered another slice of walnut-colored toast.

"You're a bright boy, Martin, an apt pupil," he said. "Not only that, but we'll do something nice for your mother, in the bargain."

Martin sipped the strong black coffee brewed by his uncle. He was not so sure that coffee was the best part of being grownup. He excused himself while he went to the refrigerator and poured a glass of milk.

"What'll we do, Uncle Jonathan?" he asked, returning to the table.

"Well," Uncle Jonathan replied, "I guess we could start in by getting a good breakfast for your folks. They'll be getting up pretty soon. Even lawyers can't sleep all day."

This proposal seemed a little tedious to Martin, but he recognized that it was a beginning. He would have preferred a more spectacular offering, especially a project that could be prosecuted outdoors.

"Okay," he said. "We can boil some eggs or something."

His uncle arched his big white eyebrows. "We'll get 'em something better than that," Uncle Jonathan declared. "We'll do everything up nice. How about pancakes?"

"Can you make pancakes?" Martin asked.

"You set the table in the dining room, Martin," said Uncle Jonathan, "and I'll mix up the best mess of flapjacks you ever saw around this house. Flapjacks and bacon and syrup, Martin! We'll show 'em something around here."

Remarkably enough, that was precisely the accomplishment that was achieved in the Butterfield household in the next hour.

When Mr. and Mrs. Butterfield came down to the kitchen, coffee was perking on the stove, bacon was staying crisp in the warming oven, and a big ladle of creamy yellow batter was laying its first pancake on the sizzling griddle.

Uncle Jonathan was so busy he could hardly look up from his work to study the surprise he had scored. Martin borrowed his uncle's attitude, and was so busy rushing china and silver back and forth from the kitchen to the dining room that he had to ask his father to step out of the way in order that breakfast preparations might proceed without unnecessary interference from onlookers.

Mrs. Butterfield, dispossessed from her own kitchen, drifted into the dining room but tactfully refrained from correcting certain disorders in the table arrangements. Mr. Butterfield left the kitchen and went to the front door to study the weather.

Martin and Uncle Jonathan remained in the kitchen, Uncle Jonathan turning the pancakes on the griddle and Martin paying him the silent homage of peering over the top of the stove and watching the cakes turn a warm lacy brown and gold.

"We sure surprised them, Uncle Jonathan," Martin said.

"They didn't know we had it in us, Martin," said Uncle Jonathan gravely.

When a good high pillar of cakes had been stacked in the warming oven, Uncle Jonathan decided he could meet the pancake demand, and breakfast was served.

Mr. and Mrs. Butterfield sat down, guests in their own house, and were soon swarmed over by two of the most attentive servants ever seen in Fern Township.

"A lawyer's got to eat plenty or he'll run out of wind in court—and wind is important to lawyers," Uncle Jonathan said with that nicety of tact for which Attorney Butterfield had often expressed ample appreciation.

"Have plenty of pancakes, Dad," Martin advised loyally. "You don't get pancakes like these around here every day."

Mr. Butterfield glanced with a sudden brightening at his wife and unloaded a stack of flapjacks onto his plate. Mrs. Butterfield eyed her son, before turning to her guest-uncle.

"They're wonderful, Uncle Jonathan," she said.

Mr. Butterfield spoke with his mouth full. "They sure are, Uncle Jonathan," he affirmed. "As Martin says, we don't get 'em as good as this every day."

"Oh, Martha can make better ones, I guess," Uncle Jonathan said, clearly meaning the exact opposite.

"You ask her," said Mr. Butterfield.

Mrs. Butterfield did not wait. "Of course I can't, Uncle Jonathan," she said firmly.

She kept eyeing Martin, however, as if somebody had stolen her first-born.

The subject of her attention was not at the moment aware of this scrutiny. Sitting behind a plate of Uncle Jonathan's flapjacks, he was quite sure that no breakfast had ever tasted so sweet, that no morning had ever been born more happily. The savory flavor of novelty was in this breakfast that he, himself, had helped to make. Furthermore he, Martin Butterfield, was learning a wonderful way to solve the ancient and irritating problem of how to get along with one's parents.

The system of doing good for one's folks had absolutely limitless possibilities. By careful use of it, a boy might possibly build up so many credits that he could do almost anything he wanted to without the subsequent unpleasantnesses that ordinarily harried him.

"Boy," he said happily, "isn't this a good breakfast?"

Mr. Butterfield laid down his fork. "As far as I can recall," the lawyer said, "this is the first time that I ever heard you mention breakfast, aside from not wanting very much."

"But this is different," Martin said.

That queer look of mild pain passed through Mrs. Butterfield's soft gray eyes again.

When breakfast was finished, Uncle Jonathan insisted on playing his rôle all the way through. He and Martin, whose enthusiasm for doing good became slightly tarnished in the face of a pile of dirty dishes, stood at the sink, washing and drying as Mr. Butterfield prepared to leave for the office.

"You can't do much today," the attorney shouted as he got his raincoat out of the hall closet. Mr. Butterfield had unwittingly stated exactly what he meant, and a challenge, to boot.

"Doesn't look like it," Uncle Jonathan replied.

"Well, you might find a good book and read awhile," Mr. Butterfield said. "Martin could afford to look in a book once in a while now that school's coming on."

Martin silently dried the plate he was holding and felt a pang.

"It's a good day for that but not much else," Uncle Jonathan assented, with at least as much enthusiasm as Martin exhibited. He added an aside for Martin's benefit, "I never was one for books."

"Neither was I," said Martin, while he finished another plate. "What can we do today when it's raining like this?"

Uncle Jonathan hummed to himself.

"We'll think of something," he said.

The "something" that Uncle Jonathan thought of was a walk in the rain. Booted and umbrellaed, he and Martin set out as soon as the dishes were done.

"You'll be glad to have us out from underfoot, Martha," Uncle Jonathan told Mrs. Butterfield.

"I do hope you won't stay out very long," she replied. "I wouldn't mind having you around the house—you wouldn't be in the way at all."

"We'd be a nuisance and you know it, Martha," Uncle Jonathan said with an impatience born more of a desire to be outside than a spirit of sacrifice. "Come on, Martin."

Leaving Mrs. Butterfield at the door, they sallied off the porch, out into the August rain, and down the avenue under the dripping lane of shade trees.

For a man who had no announced purpose in taking a walk, Uncle Jonathan showed a remarkable lack of indecision.

"Let's go down to the firehouse, Martin," he said. "There's always a bunch of good fellows around a firehouse on a rainy day."

"That's a really super idea, Uncle Jonathan," Martin replied.

"The firehouse it is, then," said Uncle Jonathan.

Being careful to walk through all the puddles and to do a little splashing with their boots, Martin and his great-uncle finally presented themselves at the door of the old red brick building in the Fern Township business district.

The big green swinging doors through which the village fire truck occasionally roared to its spectacular destinations were closed today, but the bright electric lights glowing through the windows were evidence that Uncle Jonathan knew all about firehouses.

"Do you know anybody in the firehouse?" Martin inquired of his great-uncle. He had never been allowed to play around the firehouse, unfortunately.

"Naw, but we'll get acquainted, all right," Uncle Jonathan said.

He led Martin through the small side door into the main room.

Along the wall opposite Fern Township's fiery red instrument of fire fighting, a number of chairs, in a long, neat row, were tipped back against the wall and, already on this rainy August morning, space was at a premium.

A row of graying heads, volunteer firemen all, turned to regard the newcomers.

"Good morning, men," Uncle Jonathan said breezily. "Just stopped by to look over your fire engine."

Five minutes later Uncle Jonathan had made the acquaintance of everybody in the firehouse. Somebody had rustled up a couple of chairs. Uncle Jonathan and Martin were tipped back against the wall as professionally as the most veteran chair tippers in the place.

"It was back in nineteen-and-oh-two, up in the northern part of the state, that I fought the biggest fire we ever had . . ." Uncle Jonathan was saying.

Martin cautiously balanced his chair and settled down in a quiet transport of pure joy. If he ever grew up, a process so slow it seemed it would never end, he would certainly be like Uncle Jonathan. Unlike other grown-ups, Uncle Jonathan did not waste a lot of time in an office or engage in similar monotonous affairs of grown-up people. He did the things that people *want* to do.

Martin half-closed his eyes and only half-listened to the drone of talk among the volunteer firemen and the oldest ex-volunteer ever seen in Fern Township.

He wished Sparky Roberts were around to see him sitting in a tilted chair with the *other* men, just like a real fireman. Maybe old Sparky wouldn't turn green with envy. Just maybe.

Martin was just beginning to daydream a long, fine scene in which Sparky came by the firehouse and saw him, Martin Butterfield, sitting in the driver's seat of the fire truck getting ready to drive the big engine off to save the house of Miss Georgianna Semple, the best and the most beautiful scholar of the fifth-grade-to-be of the Fern Township public school.

But his dream was interrupted by the jangle of the old phone on the wall. One of the firemen answered.

"Yeah, yeah, yeah," he said rapidly. "We're on the way, Mrs. Bussy."

Before the fireman had hung up the receiver, the row of chairs along the wall had tipped forward, spilling out a phalanx of volunteers who raced for rubber coats and helmets.

"Fire at Widow Bussy's!" shouted the fireman at the telephone, with ill-concealed delight. "Fire at Mrs. Bussy's . . ."

His words were drowned out as the siren on top of the firehouse began to emit a long wail, the result of a button being pressed somewhere in the station. The big doors of the firehouse had swung open before Martin realized that his great-uncle was hoisting him up over the side of the fire truck. Uncle Jonathan himself jumped on the side gleefully shouting, "Fire! Fire!" as the grocer, Buck Buckmaster, still in his white apron, came loping into the fire-house and leaped into the driver's seat.

With the remarkable speed that only amateur firemen can show, Fern Township's conflagration-battling department swarmed on to the truck. The big vehicle coughed, roared and rolled out of the firehouse, turning down the street toward the lower end of town where, it was hoped in certain quarters, quite a fire might be in progress.

Once on the truck and realizing that he was in no danger of being ordered off now, Martin Butterfield made his presence known to Chief Buckmaster by climbing over the stacks of hose and dropping into the front seat where the view was excellent, despite the rain beating down over the top of the windshield.

Buck Buckmaster, the grocer, was sufficiently occupied with driving the big fire truck not to notice his front-seat companion for a moment. When he did turn to find he had company, he spoke.

Said the fire chief, "Well, what do you know . . ."

Martin did not plumb the depths of meaning there might have been in this remark. Instead, he adopted an attitude of bland friendliness.

"Hello, Mr. Buckmaster," he said. "It's not a very nice day for a fire, is it?"

Mr. Buckmaster stared ahead, muttering. Martin turned and looked back at his Uncle Jonathan, who was showing himself a remarkably agile rider on the side of the truck. Hanging on to the shining silver hand rail, Uncle Jonathan nodded his head up and down vigorously, a motion that clearly meant, "Boy, this is the real stuff!"

His vigorous head bobbing also served to emphasize the fact that he had somehow acquired a red fire helmet in the midst of the confusion that occurred when the Widow Bussy's phone call came in to the firehouse.

For the moment, the souls of Martin and his great-uncle were in tune, in that harmonious unity of purpose that can befall only those human beings who take a lusty interest in the affairs of living. For the moment, both forgot their earlier resolves to patch things up with Mr. and Mrs. Butterfield.

It occurred to Martin that neither he nor Uncle Jonathan would be occupying their present exalted positions if his father had not had to drive over to the county seat that morning to try a case. As a leading volunteer fireman, Mr. Butterfield might have felt inclined to do without the assistance of this pair of fire fighters.

As the truck neared Widow Bussy's neighborhood, Martin looked for smoke blackening the sky, but the only color overhead was the leaden gray of a layer of clouds that was loosening a steady downpour of rain.

"It's not a very good day for a fire, Mr. Buckmaster," Martin observed again. "The rain's liable to put it out before we get there."

"That *is* a problem, isn't it?" Mr. Buckmaster answered with a startled sidewise glance.

Martin was pleased that he had been able to contribute an idea to the morning's sport, even though it was a rather discouraging thought.

Women appeared on porches, and children, bareheaded in the rain, stared from front walks as the Fern Township Volunteer Fire Department rounded the corner and rolled into Widow Bussy's street.

Buck Buckmaster expertly wheeled the truck up to the fire plug nearest the Bussy residence and halted. Martin rose in his place and now, at closer range, joyfully discerned certain strands of pale bluish smoke hanging about the roof of the Bussy house.

Mrs. Bussy was nowhere in sight.

Martin's survey of the situation was ended by sudden activity on the truck. A handful of volunteers began to unroll the big canvas-rubber water hose and race toward the fire hydrant, while yet another group started to spin out the thinner, snakier hose of the truck's chemical tank, rushing down the sidewalk toward the Bussy home.

The spindle jammed and pulled the chemical party up short, Chief Buckmaster skidding undignifiedly to his knees in the wet grass along the sidewalk. This incident was fortunate because it permitted Uncle Jonathan to overtake and pass this fleet party of firemen.

"Come on, Martin!" he shouted, "you and I better get up there to the house and get ready for the firemen when they get that hose loose."

Martin lost no time in following his great-uncle, who showed respectable speed for his years.

It was not until Uncle Jonathan had climbed the front steps of Mrs. Bussy's house that Martin saw that his relative was really an experienced fireman. Uncle Jonathan had peeled a fire ax off the side of the truck.

As Martin reached the top step, he realized that he was about to witness the most fascinating aspect of fire fighting known to small boys.

"They're going to be in a hurry, can't lose any time," Uncle Jonathan shouted. "Stand back."

With a well-aimed and altogether wonderful swing of the ax, Uncle Jonathan struck the upper hinge of Widow Bussy's old oak front door. It was surprising how the dust flew out of the ancient door jamb and how the whole door dropped inward with a quiet, tired creak.

Uncle Jonathan had knocked the door down with a single blow. He dropped his ax and rushed inside the house.

Martin paused only long enough to pick up the ax and knock the other hinge off. It came off easily.

Then he plunged into the house to sniff a satisfyingly smoky smell. He followed the dim figure of his great-uncle through the smoke-clouded rooms of the house to the kitchen, where the Widow Bussy was struggling with her big black wood stove.

"Flue's on fire," that brisk householder announced calmly. "Where are those lazy loafers of firemen?"

Her question was immediately answered when, out of nowhere, Buck Buckmaster appeared.

"Oh—oh, the flue!" he diagnosed accurately. "I'll send a couple of guys up on the roof."

In a moment there was the sound of a ladder hitting the sloping back porch roof and then there were the scratchings and strugglings of firemen up above. Martin saw a hose dangling past a window and he started toward the back door. He had no doubt his uncle would want to fight the fire on the roof.

But Uncle Jonathan, strangely subdued, remained standing by the kitchen stove.

"Heck, a flue fire," he said. "I thought it might be worth coming to."

The Widow Bussy was by no means so fragile a soul that she let the excitement of the moment soften her belligerent attitude toward the world at large.

She turned from the smoking plates of her stove long enough to favor Uncle Jonathan with a withering smile.

"Aren't you the old character that's visiting the Butterfields?" she inquired. "What do you want—a widow's house burned down?"

She was holding a lid tool while she talked, and Uncle Jonathan eyed it as a possible weapon.

"That's gratitude for you," Uncle Jonathan replied mildly. "Here we come rushing out to save a woman's house and . . ."

He turned to Martin.

"Let's not stay where we're not wanted, Martin," he said.

Martin and Uncle Jonathan went outside into the back yard where the view of the fire fighting was better anyway, leaving Mrs. Bussy in the kitchen.

Outside, Martin and his great-uncle peered up on the shingled roof where hose was strung and where firemen clambered around the flue, tearing up a few shingles and peering down into the holes thus made.

"Nothing duller than a flue fire," remarked Uncle Jonathan.

"Oh, it's not so bad," Martin said.

With the air of a couple of critics reviewing a new play, they stood in the rain and watched. It was wet and cold and both of them would have welcomed a quick return to the firehouse.

Firemen climbed up and down, looking into the chimney and checking on the stove and the stovepipes.

When Buck Buckmaster started up for the last time, Uncle Jonathan spoke to him.

"Guess we got 'er licked, Buck," he said.

Buck looked over his shoulder as he climbed the ladder.

"Guess so," he said.

The chief had just reached the roof line of the porch when the Widow Bussy's voice could be heard distantly but clearly from the house. It was not a call—rather it was a mixture of a battle cry and a shriek.

Transfixed on the ladder, Buck Buckmaster turned and looked down at Uncle Jonathan and Martin.

"What was that?" he asked in the silence that fell suddenly.

"Don't know," Uncle Jonathan answered, "but it sounded like that crazy woman who seems to own this house . . ."

164

While they speculated, the back screen door of the house burst open.

The Widow Bussy made a remarkable figure carrying a fire ax.

The sight caused Martin Butterfield to have an uneasy feeling in the pit of his stomach. But he looked up at his great-uncle, who was taking in the picture with calm, intense, untroubled interest.

Martin felt better; after all, this was a fire. There couldn't be any trouble about an old door.

On the porch Widow Bussy stood uncertainly for a moment and the sound she made, Uncle Jonathan said later, resembled remarkably the cry of a coyote on a moonlit night —and was just as silly, he added.

Mrs. Bussy looked up at Chief Buckmaster so speculatively that the grocer-fire chief came down the ladder hurriedly before any plan to chop the legs off that piece of equipment could be carried out.

"Where'd you get that fire ax?" the chief asked meekly.

Martin nudged his elderly relative.

"Let's go back and get on the truck, Uncle Jonathan," he suggested.

"In a minute," said Uncle Jonathan. "She seems to be awful piqued, don't she?"

If Widow Bussy had been merely piqued a moment before, Chief Buckmaster's query about the ax changed all that.

"You should ask!" she shouted. "Smashing up my front door! You—you—you—!"

Chief Buckmaster, understandably, was thunderstruck. He leaned against the ladder and his honest face was as nearly blank as the human countenance is likely to get.

"Maybe we *ought* to get back on the truck, now that you mention it," Uncle Jonathan said to Martin.

His movement was a mistake.

The Widow Bussy's suspicions naturally and, for once truly, leaped right to a bull's-eye—the nearest person that she happened to be at war with.

"Somebody smashed my front door," she yelled, pointing at Uncle Jonathan.

While Chief Buckmaster looked on in awe, Uncle Jonathan turned to the Widow Bussy.

"Madam," he said with a certain oratorical flourish, "you are quite right about the door. In a fire, the firemen must not be delayed."

The Widow Bussy accepted this statement of logic with a lack of understanding that was embarrassing.

Martin felt sorry that anybody could be so dumb.

The widow suddenly waved the ax. "That front door wasn't locked!" she cried.

Buck Buckmaster looked up on the roof where all fire operations had ceased while the firemen listened. "We didn't even go in the front door," he mused.

"No," said Uncle Jonathan, "but you might've—you might've."

Martin Butterfield saw the force of this lucid reasoning strike home. Chief Buckmaster looked as if he, not the door, had been tapped by a fire ax.

The chief said something to Widow Bussy in a low voice, then assisted her into the house, quieting and shushing her warlike mutterings.

The firemen went back to work, and presently the Volunteer Fire Department of Fern Township, including Uncle Jonathan and Martin, was returning from its fire-fighting job with a certain rising hilarity.

By the time they reached the firehouse, Uncle Jonathan had become a kind of hero or something, Martin noticed.

They were calling him The Hatchetman.

It was sure great to have an uncle who could do anything —and let you help him, in the bargain.

That night at the Butterfields, Martin went to bed early again.

For some reason or other, Mr. Butterfield came home from work not feeling so well. It was one of those phenomena known in the Butterfield household as "a bad day at the office."

Mr. Butterfield took Martin aside before bedtime, however.

"Martin," he asked, "how did Uncle Jonathan happen to break down a door at Widow Bussy's today?"

"How?" Martin echoed. "Why, with a big old fire ax, that's how."

Mr. Butterfield studied his son with a preoccupied look.

Martin amplified his previous statement. "I helped him," he said. "And you know what?"

"What?" asked Mr. Butterfield.

"Mrs. Bussy got awful mad just when we were trying to help her get her old fire out."

Mr. Butterfield mumbled quietly to himself.

After Martin was in bed, he could hear Uncle Jonathan talking to his father and mother in the living room.

Uncle Jonathan was laughing and once he shouted, "Sure, I'll pay for it, George! Doggone it, it was good just to get a fire ax in my paws again—hanged if it wasn't!"

Martin fell asleep hoping that his uncle would stay in Fern Township forever.

But his hope was not to be fulfilled. In fact, it was to fall very far short. Uncle Jonathan concluded his visit to the Butterfields the next afternoon—with that boyish suddenness with which he did everything.

"Can't be bothering my relatives forever," he said at the lunch table.

"You're no trouble," Mrs. Butterfield said pleasantly.

Martin could not speak; his sorrow, however, was softened by the presentation of a dollar bill, a half-dollar, a quarter, a dime, a nickel, and a penny. "Samples of the coin of the realm," Uncle Jonathan said.

Mr. Butterfield suddenly began to eat a hearty lunch. He concealed his grief very well.

When the afternoon train had gone, Mr. Butterfield stood on the Fern Township platform with his wife and son, watching the train's smoke plume diminish down the tracks in the distance.

Then he looked down at Martin.

"Well, Martin," he said gaily. "A few more days and you'll be back in school."

Martin jingled the money in his pocket. He had a few days, at least, in which to enjoy being alive. That was something.

"Yes, sir," he said meekly.

CHAPTER 10

Reluctantly to School

ON THE first Tuesday after Labor Day, the great cycle of the seasons in all its majesty closed in on the small figure of Martin Butterfield. Like all the other boys in Fern Township, Martin was helpless before the unrelenting and powerful forces of all the world combined. In short, Martin went back to school.

In doing so, he became for the first time a fifth grader in the rambling big wooden building that housed the young scholars of the village. This was an upward step on the ladder of life, but Martin eyed it with suspicion solely because so many people assured him that he *would* like it.

"There's nothing like education, Martin," his father told him gravely.

Martin agreed with this contention, of course, but in a way that he felt might be better left unexpressed.

"And you're going to have Miss Gillis again," his mother, who was president of the Parent-Teachers' Association, added. "Miss Gillis will teach fifth grade this year, instead of fourth."

"Heck!" Martin exclaimed. "I thought I was through with Miss Gillis."

His impulse on the subject of Miss Gillis had nothing whatever to do with the ability, efficiency, character or appearance of Miss Gillis, who scored high on all counts. Rather, it sprang from the fact that, to boys like Martin, it was occasionally a nice thing to have a teacher who knew nothing of their prior scholastic efforts.

It was a fine, sunny morning the day after Labor Day.

Why must it always be sunny on the day school starts? Martin asked himself as he walked up the avenue and whistled up Sparky Roberts. Why can't there be rain and lightning and thunder so you wouldn't want to be outside anyway?

Sparky Roberts bounced off the front porch of the Roberts home, scrubbed and brushed and wearing a new set of corduroy slacks that were identical to Martin's, along with a shirt that was so similar it suggested that Martin and Sparky had been together when shopping with their mothers for school.

"Hi, Martin," Sparky said. "Do your old pants make a good swish when you walk?"

Martin and Sparky practiced walking with their legs close together, listening to the swishes.

"Some pants," said Martin. "I got a new belt."

He lifted his blouse and revealed this item.

"That's nothing," replied Sparky. He lifted *his* blouse. A new leather belt circled his waist.

"I got a quarter," Martin said.

"What for?" Sparky asked.

"Just nothin'," Martin replied airily.

"Lemme see it."

"If you don't believe it, you don't need to see it."

"You want to start something, Martin?"

"Do you want to get them new pants all tore up?"

"Who's going to . . .?"

This interesting dialog carried the two young seekers after knowledge up to the corner opposite Fern Township school.

On the curb waiting to cross when the schoolboy patrolman gave the sign was Georgianna Semple, the golden-haired child of fifth grade, the single attractive aspect of education that Martin had encountered in school.

Georgianna was starched to such an extent that she appeared to be sprouting wings. Her hair glistened from brushing. She looked shyly at Martin Butterfield and Sparky Roberts as they unavoidably drew even with her.

Martin and Sparky had already observed Georgianna but, from their manner, it would have been easy to draw the conclusion that neither was aware any girl was within a mile.

On the corner, Sparky shoved Martin. Martin shoved Sparky. The result was a mild wrestling match on the curb before the eyes of the best scholar in the fifth grade.

The traffic patrolman, a tiny fourth-grader, said, "Stay on the curb until I tell you to go."

"We'll go if we want to," Sparky replied with a boldness that should have impressed any feminine heart.

"And nobody can stop us," Martin added, in sudden loyalty to his late adversary.

Martin and Sparky stepped tentatively down off the curb and thereby achieved the feat of getting into difficulties with the Educational System before they even arrived at the scene where learning was dealt out.

Georgianna Semple elevated her pretty nose and walked off alone as soon as the traffic congestion was cleared at the corner.

Around the school, small rivers of children flowed and coursed under the trees, and Georgianna Semple disappeared into the panorama of bright printed cottons, blouses, skirts and jumpers.

"See what you did?" Martin said to Sparky. "Now Miss Gillis will be mad at us before we start."

"You did it as much as I did," Sparky replied.

When the school bell rang, they were on the end of the line that marched briskly down the main corridor to the fifth-grade classroom.

Miss Gillis, a tall, dark-haired, pretty girl, was waiting at the door as they passed. She had talked to the tiny patrolman. But she was willing to forgive.

"Now, let's start the new year right, boys," she said gently as she closed in behind the marching phalanx of the fifth grade.

"Yes, ma'am," Martin and Sparky replied solemnly.

Once inside their new home room, both boys grabbed back seats, but Miss Gillis did not need to look at her seating chart to alter these arrangements. The first pupils to be honored with permanent desks, after the class had sung "America," pledged allegiance to the flag, and performed its other morning preliminaries, were Martin Butterfield and Sparky Roberts. The two found themselves occupying the front seats closest to Miss Gillis herself.

Martin Butterfield made one meek offer.

"Somebody else that has to wear glasses can have this seat if he wants it, Miss Gillis," he said. "I can see fine from the back."

"So can I," said Sparky.

"That's awfully nice of you," Miss Gillis replied, "but I'm sure we'll work it out somehow."

Once the scholars were settled, Miss Gillis sat down at her desk in the front of the room and made a little speech of welcome. Miss Gillis was young and, she loved her work and she loved the children and she was anxious that all of them get everything possible out of her teaching.

"Now that we're fifth-graders," she said, "we're all a little bigger and a little older so we ought to be a little better, isn't that true?" Some heads nodded.

Miss Gillis went on while Martin's attention gradually focused on the ceiling where, he discovered, the carpenters had been at work during the summer vacation.

The ceiling was covered with sound-proofing and the sound-proofing was simply full of tiny little holes arranged in perfect squares.

Martin immediately slumped in his seat, as if he were engaging in profound thought, and began to count the holes. It was better than doing nothing.

How long he counted before he realized he was being spoken to, he did not know. He was up to 279 on the fourth square when he heard his name drifting down upon his ears. Automatically, he sat up.

"Yes, ma'am," he said.

Miss Gillis was looking at him. Sparky Roberts was looking at him. The rest of the class was looking at him.

"Your eyes were open, Martin," Miss Gillis said.

Martin felt a slow blush come up over his hot cheeks. He said nothing. In dealing with educational authorities, he had found silence a golden course.

"You must pay better attention," Miss Gillis advised in a friendly manner, this being the first day of school and therefore a little early for penalties and punishment.

Martin sat up straighter in his seat. Fifth grade, he decided, bore a remarkable resemblance to fourth grade, just as fourth had to third.

Miss Gillis looked at him again to make sure that his affairs were in order and then, for the first time, Martin paid her sufficient attention to learn what she had been discussing.

". . . now we're going to be very grown-up," Miss Gillis said. "And there will be a prize for the pupil who does the best work and gets the best grades."

This prospect seemed to Martin to be gross discrimination. He could see Miss Georgianna Semple right now getting the old prize, whatever it was, and . . .

Miss Gillis went on. She shook a graceful finger at the class and smiled her prettiest smile.

"But there will be another prize, too," she said. "This year we're going to have a prize for the pupil who shows the most improvement in his work—that gives every single one of us a chance, doesn't it?"

Martin Butterfield had no trouble focusing his attention upon *this* proposal.

Before he realized what he was doing, his eyes drifted dreamily to the ceiling where he saw a wonderful picture —Martin and Georgianna standing before the fifth grade class and proudly being awarded a . . . a . . .

He hadn't heard what the prize was to be. With a sudden and complete new interest in educational affairs, he leaned over to Sparky Roberts. "What do you get if you win?" he whispered.

"*You* don't get nothin'," Sparky replied before this exchange was cut off by Miss Gillis.

"If you two boys will wait just a moment," she said, while the class tittered appreciatively, "I'll tell everybody what the prize is. The prize will be—" she paused, as if it made even a grown person breathless to think of it, "—the prize will be a trip to Washington. I'll take the winners myself on Thanksgiving."

The class murmured with the kind of murmur that was expected of it and most of the expression was genuine.

The murmur changed into a minor clamor.

Martin received the tidings with mixed feelings. Washington was far away and therefore a very desirable place to visit, in his opinion. On the other hand, Thanksgiving was far away, too. The rigors of improving steadily from now to Thanksgiving would, Martin estimated, put him into a class reserved for angels and other people whose professions seemed less than adventurous.

Martin wriggled in his seat and tentatively dipped his little finger into his inkwell to find out whether there was any ink in it. There was. He idly drew a heavy blue line across the top of his desk. Then he looked over at Sparky Roberts.

In that instant he caught Sparky looking speculatively at him. Before Sparky could adopt an air of complete detachment about such childish affairs as prizes, Martin knew with positive certainty that Sparky Roberts had conceived some idea that *he* was going to win the trip to Washington. Even if Martin had utterly despised trips to Washington, it was now impossible for him to reach any honorable decision except that he should be the winner of the big trip.

He too adopted a careless, disarming attitude. Looking at him, it might have been suspected that he was against taking a trip anywhere, even to Africa to hunt lions with Frank Buck.

At the very moment he presented this aspect, Martin Butterfield was making a resolution. When Miss Gillis took the prize scholars to Washington, he would be one of them just as certainly as Georgianna would be the other.

He would improve and improve and improve . . .

Martin Butterfield had an electric inspiration. He paused.

He leaned back in his seat and his eyes drifted upward toward the ceiling again, at the countless but wonderfully countable holes in the sound-proofing.

In a contest like this, there would be a distinct advantage in starting from nothing. It was pure, clean logic. Martin Butterfield decided to seize the bottom of the scholastic ladder so firmly that no other boy in the fifth grade could possibly wrest it away from him. Once established in this happy low estate, he would have a much longer way to climb than anybody unfortunate enough to occupy the higher rungs of fifth-grade scholarship.

Martin sat up at his desk, folded his hands neatly in front of him and suddenly took a vital interest in the affairs of fifth grade.

Martin and Sparky tucked their arithmetic books under their respective belts as soon as the last afternoon bell freed them from school that afternoon.

Neither of them carried more than one book, although Georgianna Semple found it necessary to take all of hers home. When Martin and Sparky emerged from the school door into the shaded playground, Georgianna was carefully stacking the heavy load of volumes on her big geography.

The boys recognized the opportunity simultaneously.

"I'll help you with your old books," Martin said carelessly.

"I can carry more books than anybody, I guess," Sparky said.

"Maybe I can carry them," Georgianna replied, but she did not resist. Her books were instantly divided and carried by two Samaritans who gave every evidence of doing only that which they would have done for anyone with too many books to carry.

With Georgianna between them, still starched, still glistening after a day in school, Martin and Sparky walked slowly down the street.

"Isn't it wonderful about the trip to Washington?" Georgianna asked.

Martin waited to find out what Sparky would say but Sparky cautiously said nothing.

"Don't you think it's wonderful, Martin?" Georgianna persisted.

"You mean about the trip?" Martin parried.

"Why, of course," she exclaimed and her little peal of laughter was both beautiful and cruel.

"What did you think she meant?" Sparky inquired scornfully.

"Oh," Martin said aimlessly, "I guess it will be all right."

Georgianna stopped abruptly on the sidewalk. "All right?" she said. "Why, it's just wonderful. Think of going all the way to Washington with Miss Gillis and seeing everything and things!"

She sighed a truly deep sigh for the wonders of the world that were now held out to the whole fifth grade.

"I guess it's no bigger than New York," Martin said.

"You ever been to New York?" Sparky inquired.

"I was talking to Georgianna," said Martin.

Georgianna walked primly between her two porters.

They walked her all the way to her front hedge and then delivered up her books reluctantly.

"Where are *your* books?" she asked, as if the missing volumes had not come to her attention before.

Each boy rapped his stomach.

"My gracious," the best scholar in the grade said admiringly, "I don't see how you can get along with only one book."

Martin and Sparky both felt a certain male superiority as they walked off down the street together.

They parted in front of Martin's house, after a long conference on when, where, and how they should meet again.

It was decided that, barring maternal interference, they would rendezvous in the barn as soon as they changed their clothes. After the briefest of conversations with their respective mothers, Martin and Sparky repaired to the Butterfield barn, where Martin found a ball of light chalk line that he had lost a year before.

Supplied with this minor bit of inspiration, Martin and Sparky spent the remaining hours before dinner time constructing a box kite to catch the winds of September. Before the suddenly urgent need of a kite, the problems of education evaporated wispily into nowhere.

Mr. Butterfield did not pick up the evening paper immediately after dinner that night.

Instead, he and Martin went to the living room for a good man-to-man talk while Mrs. Butterfield considerately kept her distance in the kitchen, doing the dishes.

Mr. Butterfield appeared to be uncertain in his rôle as mentor; nevertheless, he was willing to discharge his parental duties conscientiously. He settled in the big wing chair and Martin sat on the davenport.

It was a serious occasion and Martin sensed its sobriety.

"How did it go at school today?" Mr. Butterfield began.

"All right," Martin replied.

"When you get to fifth grade, Martin," his father continued, "you had better begin to take your lessons seriously. Fifth grade is a pretty high grade."

Martin searched his mind for some adequate reply.

"It's all right," he said.

"Was it interesting, Martin?"

Martin thought a moment. He had better not mention the competition for a trip to Washington just yet, he guessed. His father might not understand.

"It was all right," Martin said stoutly.

Mr. Butterfield looked pained. "Can't you say anything but all right?" he inquired.

Martin wriggled on the sofa. "I have some arithmetic to do," he said. "Maybe I ought to be getting at it."

For the first time, Mr. Butterfield took some satisfaction from his little conference with his heir. Or perhaps it was only relief at having an excuse to conclude his duties as a parent.

"That's fine," he said, picking up the paper. "And remember, Martin, I want to get good reports on your work at school."

Martin slid down off the davenport.

"I'll try to improve, Dad," he said.

Mr. Butterfield looked at Martin piercingly for a moment before unfolding the evening paper. "That's the stuff," he said.

Martin improved the next hour by sitting in his room upstairs whittling carefully on four long sticks of balsa wood that were destined to go into one of the strongest, lightest box kites ever seen in Fern Township.

His glistening new red arithmetic book lay open before him but the problems remained unsolved. Improvement, Martin figured, should not even *begin* to set in for a week or so. He whittled away busily, occasionally stopping to brush the shavings off the unstudied pages.

By the middle of the second day of school, Martin Butterfield had achieved the distinction of earning an unadulterated zero in every recitation period, while Georgianna Semple made a record that was exactly the opposite.

It was not so simple to do as Martin had imagined. It was sometimes difficult to pass up opportunities to raise one's hand and answer the easy questions; but Martin was forbearing.

Perhaps it was his forbearance that undid him.

One of Miss Gillis' strong points as a teacher was that

she took as much delight in bringing the "slow" student along as she did in observing the progress of the bright little stars in her scholastic firmament.

As the day wore on, she became more and more concerned for Martin Butterfield.

In afternoon reading period, when Martin seemed to have trouble reading such difficult words as "the" and "and," she paused in her flight.

"Are you sure you feel all right, Martin?" she inquired.

"I feel fine," Martin assured her.

Miss Gillis sat at her desk and pondered.

"All right," she said, "we'll go over the lesson again, then."

Martin, who was not yet ready for improvement, did not improve on the second reading.

Miss Gillis listened with the pain that only a truly conscientious young teacher can feel.

When Martin sat down, she shook her head.

"Martin, you'll have to study hard and improve . . ." she began.

Her long lashes suddenly opened wide in self-startlement, which she concealed as quickly as the blush faded from her cheeks.

"Sparky Roberts," she said, "will you read, please?"

A flash of inspiration touched Sparky Roberts also. He promptly and clearly made a zero for himself in reading. Three other boys in the fifth-grade reading class followed suit.

Martin Butterfield, looking into his book with beautifully concentrated interest, wondered, then worried, then knew.

Every boy in the class had suddenly discovered Martin's technique. Every boy in the class was ready to enter the self-improvement contest now, beginning, of course, with the worst exhibition possible.

Miss Gillis had the grace to know not only when a high purpose had been defeated but also when she had invited such a defeat. For the remainder of the class period, she called only on little girls; little girls, at least, could be expected to be—to be—well, civilized.

Miss Gillis' faith in her own powers was shaken, as far as boys went.

The same could be said for Martin Butterfield. Sitting in his conspicuous seat up in the front, he followed the reading lesson with an air of perfect intentness while he turned over in his mind certain statements he planned to make to Sparky Roberts concerning copycats. If Sparky couldn't think up a good way to win the scholarship contest, then he should at least be man enough not to horn into somebody else's business.

Martin would have executed his plan of operation on Sparky immediately after school let out, except for one minor mischance. Miss Gillis asked Martin to remain after the last period.

Martin wriggled in his seat as his more fortunate mates put their papers away, packed up their books and filed out of the room under the guidance of Miss Gillis. Martin peeked out the window toward freedom long enough to observe Sparky Roberts going down the street with Georgianna.

He felt very much alone when Miss Gillis returned.

Miss Gillis sat down at her desk. She looked at Martin and suddenly her pretty eyes were large with tears.

For the first time in his life, Martin felt the deep trouble that a woman's tears can inflict upon the male, large or small.

Miss Gillis reached for her lacy handkerchief and Martin found himself instinctively using the ancient formula. He stood up and cleared his throat.

"Don't cry, Miss Gillis," he said.

His voice sounded very large in the empty schoolroom.

Miss Gillis paused in her quiet eye dabbing. "I thought it was such a *good* idea, Martin," she whispered. "I thought that everybody would pitch in and improve —"

Martin stood erect. He could not afford to be less than manly before a lady in distress. That was the way men were supposed to be.

"I *will* improve, Miss Gillis," he assured her solemnly. "But first I got to —"

It was a mistake.

"First," said Miss Gillis, "you must upset the whole fifth grade, Martin!"

This had been the least of Martin Butterfield's intentions.

"Oh, no," he replied earnestly. "Those other boys— they're just a bunch of copycats. They can't ever think of anything to do for themselves, Miss Gillis."

Miss Gillis stopped her eye dabbing altogether.

Martin had scored a point. After all, it was *his* plan and he had not engaged in incitement to rebellion; quite to the contrary, mass rebellion was the last thing he wanted.

For some reason or other, Miss Gillis could find nothing to say except "Oh!"

Finally, after a thoughtful pause, she asked, "When do you plan to begin improving, Martin?"

Martin looked down at his toes and then up at the ceiling.

"I guess," he said slowly, "I can start pretty soon now. If I started pretty soon, it would count as improvement, wouldn't it?"

"Yes, Martin," Miss Gillis said desperately. "It will count as improvement if you start tomorrow."

Martin was still not fully convinced. "Even if I got zeroes for only two days so far?" he inquired pointedly.

"Even so," Miss Gillis said.

Martin began to feel better. "Sparky Roberts didn't get as many zeroes yet as I did, did he?" he inquired.

Miss Gillis consulted her record book.

"*Nobody* got as many zeroes as you did, Martin," she said with quiet pleasure, as if she were informing him that he had made a straight "A" record.

"Well, then . . ." Martin ruminated, "I guess I can start improving tomorrow."

Miss Gillis did not smile as she nodded.

"You may go home now, Martin," she said.

"Thank you, Miss Gillis," Martin replied.

He paused beside his desk to dig out every book he owned.

Miss Gillis watched him silently.

He turned to go.

"I'm glad you stopped crying, Miss Gillis," Martin said.

Then, squaring his shoulders, he picked up his books and marched out of the room.

The school grounds were empty when he passed out the door into the shaded playground, but Martin began to whistle as he reached the street corner.

Miss Gillis had not been mad at him. She had not even written a note to his father. And she understood everything now. He was sorry she had cried like that. He kind of liked her, even though she was a schoolteacher.

He whistled contentedly to himself as he walked down the street, his armload of books braced against his hip.

When he passed Sparky Roberts' house, a footpad was waiting behind the hedge.

Sparky leaped out with both hands cocked and aimed like pistols at Martin.

"What'd she do, Martin?" he shouted. "What'd she do, huh?"

"What did who do?" Martin inquired distantly.

"You know who—Miss Gillis," said Sparky, falling into step with Martin.

"She didn't do anything," Martin said. "We just talked, me and Miss Gillis."

"What have you got all your books for?" Sparky inquired, letting his curiosity try another angle of attack.

"What for?" repeated Martin. "To study, that's what for. Didn't you ever hear of anybody going to school to learn something?"

Martin, it will be understood, had undergone a quick transformation that—for this moment, at least—was very real to him. In the few minutes that had passed while he walked from the school, he had accomplished that wonderful feat of youth—a complete change of heart. It was as real to him as if he had never felt otherwise.

He had already begun to think of himself as an earnest seeker after knowledge—even though he had not yet actively begun his search.

Sparky walked in silence beside this figure of righteousness for half a block.

"Let's go down to your barn and finish our kite," he said finally.

Martin thought a moment. "I haven't got time," he said. "I have to do my lessons."

"Holy smoke!" said Sparky Roberts.

At the next corner, Sparky Roberts' course diverged from Martin's.

"Don't wear your eyes out reading your old books!" he shouted over his shoulder.

"You're just ashamed 'cause you haven't got your books home to study," retorted the student. "Ya-ah!"

Martin drew a deep breath and was about to emit another loud coyote call when Good Fortune descended to sit upon his slender young shoulders.

Down the street, Martin perceived the approaching figure of Georgianna Semple, carrying a small parcel of groceries.

Martin's step quickened, then perceptibly slowed, as he took his surprise and pleasure simultaneously in hand.

He saw Georgianna slow down, too.

He slowed down still more. So did Georgianna.

When Martin reached her, he stopped and Georgianna stopped, too.

"Hello, Georgianna," Martin said.

"Hello, Martin," said Georgianna. "Are you just getting home from school?"

Martin blushed. "Yeah," he said, "Miss Gillis and I were —we were talking quite a while."

Georgianna smiled with a certain trace of slyness.

"She wasn't mad at me," Martin hastened to explain, even though he had not been asked.

Georgianna shifted her parcel of groceries from one arm to the other and lifted her long lashes for only a moment, but it was long enough for Martin to know he had just been bathed in a glance of feminine admiration.

"I'll carry those groceries, Georgianna," Martin offered.

Georgianna demurred. "You have your books to carry," she said. "Gracious, you really *do* have all your books, Martin!"

Martin shrugged off this astonished comment.

"I thought I'd study tonight," he explained. "But I can still carry that stuff, Georgianna."

A moment later, Martin had the bag of groceries in one arm, the books on his hip, and was walking slowly toward Georgianna's house, enjoying the delicious confidence of the most beautiful scholar in his grade.

"You aren't afraid of the teacher at all, are you, Martin?" Georgianna asked, with the furtive admiration of timid woman for reckless man.

Martin remained modestly silent for a moment. "I guess I like Miss Gillis all right," he said, as if that explained something.

"You should study harder then, Martin," Georgianna admonished him.

"I'm going to," Martin said. "See these books?"

He jiggled the books on his hip, as strong evidence of his intention.

Georgianna again lifted her eyelashes to him admiringly.

"My!" she said. Into the simple little word, she put the honest wonder she felt for the remarkable nature of Martin Butterfield, who could change for the better so suddenly.

The spirit of humility that had come to dwell in Martin did not let such an opportunity pass ungrasped.

"If you would help me, Georgianna," he said with meekness, "I might be—I might be a better boy, I guess."

Georgianna was not so young as to be untouched by such a flattering compliment.

"The very minute I get home," she said, "I'll ask my mother if you can come over to my house after supper to study with me."

Martin Butterfield walked the rest of the way to Georgianna's house and then he ran the remainder of his course home. He could not remember afterwards that his feet touched the ground.

For dessert that evening Mrs. Butterfield served the dish whose succulence was prized above all others by the sweet-toothed men of the Butterfield household—butterscotch pie.

Martin watched his mother as she set the deep dish, topped by foaming golden meringue, on the table and prepared to cut out big wedges.

The pie offered a wonderful chance to make his father and mother aware of his new grasp of matters educational.

Martin looked up at his mother.

"Mother," he said, "I don't know whether I can wait for pie. I have to get at my lessons—over at Georgianna Semple's house."

The knife hung above the pie for just a fraction of an instant.

"Did Georgianna ask you, Martin?" Mrs. Butterfield inquired with surprise.

"Yes, Mother," said Martin. "She thinks we could help each other in our work."

"I'll be blessed," said Mr. Butterfield.

Martin basked in the pleasure of the sensation he had caused, but only until his father introduced a hard note of reality.

"Well," Mr. Butterfield said, "if Martin doesn't want any pie, that leaves two pieces for me."

"Well, maybe I'll have time to eat one piece," Martin said quickly.

Mrs. Butterfield's knife descended into the creamy meringue.

Martin ate one piece of butterscotch pie and then was prevailed upon to eat yet a second.

Mr. and Mrs. Butterfield regarded this process with satisfaction. For their part, after ten years with Martin, life would have become dull if genuine, lasting reform were to set in, if Martin were suddenly to quit living for each moment as it came.

Martin meanwhile savored the sweetness of the pie. He sat quietly serene in his place. The good things of the world, it seemed tonight, were just too many to count.

CHAPTER 11

The Improvement of Martin Butterfield

I F A CHART had been drawn of the Improvement of Martin Butterfield in that autumn of his fifth-grade year, it would have shown some very interesting ups and downs that have no parallel in such fields as the Cycle of Business, the Growth of Population, or the Annual Rainfall.

Martin's chart would have shown a very sharp climb for a full week after he was "kept in" by Miss Gillis. It would not have shown, of course, the beaming satisfaction that Miss Gillis took each day in seeing Martin hand in his homework on time, recite answers to questions in a manner that allowed at least a reasonable suspicion that he had looked in the book the night before, and restrain himself from such activities as counting the pinholes in the ceiling, making paper airplanes surreptitiously under his desk, or committing himself to other pursuits that would indicate he was not wholly devoted to education.

The Chart of the Improvement of Martin Butterfield would have shown another interesting thing. For at least a week after his great climb, he stayed up there. It was not a coincidence that during this week he was the guest of Miss Georgianna Semple each evening. Georgianna, for the second whole week, devoted herself to a great project of her own. Without knowing it, she had taken on the historic task of womanhood—she was trying to make something good and useful of the reluctant male.

"Martin means well," she explained to her mother while she waited, books spread out before her, for his arrival one evening. "And if I can help him to be a good boy, I ought to, don't you think?"

"It's very good of you," Mrs. Semple smiled upon her daughter. "I only hope . . ."

She left the sentence hanging in mid-air, to the puzzlement of her daughter, and then went off to the kitchen to do the interminable tasks that grown-ups do in the household. Georgianna thought no more about it.

Georgianna continued her efforts at doing good with Martin for that whole week.

Then the Chart of the Improvement of Martin Butterfield fell off a little. For one thing, Sparky Roberts got a new Erector set that had a motor with it; the most fascinating things, including a power-driven windmill, could be built with it by two earnest and hard-working boys in the course of a long evening.

For another thing, the subject of all this improvement suddenly discovered that it is a very long time between September and November. Like a race horse with a long course ahead, Martin found it convenient to save his strength.

Thus the Chart of the Improvement of Martin Butterfield showed a drop in September and a level plateau thereafter that extended into November.

This long, level plateau was perhaps higher than the one on which Martin Butterfield had dwelt previously at school, but it was not so high that it caused its occupant to strain for scholastic breath in the rarified atmosphere.

Furthermore, it allowed him to spend his time on such autumnal occupations as football and trapping, and plain loafing in the lazy, golden days of Indian summer.

It was not until early in November that the competitive spirit was reawakened in Martin Butterfield, or, for that matter, in any boy in the fifth grade.

The reason was simple and clear: A trip to Washington within a matter of weeks was much more stimulating than a possible trip to the moon two months off. Any young male in the fifth grade could have explained that.

It happened on a Monday morning, a morning when the sky was gray and heavy and the air carried a frosty nip that promised an early snow.

Martin was deeply settled in his seat, which was still the front seat, despite his modest improvement, and Miss Gillis was at the blackboard, explaining certain very vague matters concerning fractions in arithmetic.

Martin looked out the window at the gray, crisp day, a fine day for hunting rabbits or for running a trap line. Maybe it would snow, he pondered, and then you could track animals in the woods. The tracking of animals in the woods led Martin to a logical and highly fascinating scene: A tableau in which Martin Butterfield, single-handed, had tracked and treed a large brown bear which was about to . . .

What it was about to do, Martin was not to find out, at least not that morning.

From a great distance he heard his name being spoken. The distance suddenly shrank to a few feet.

"Martin Butterfield," said Miss Gillis, "I do wish you would pay attention."

"I wasn't doing anything," Martin said.

Which was the truth.

Miss Gillis put down the chalk and suspended whatever it was she had been explaining. She passed her long, graceful fingers over her shiny hair.

Martin sat up straight in his seat and, with more intensity than mathematical understanding, studied the fractions chalked on the blackboard. Sparky Roberts shifted expectantly in his seat, a fact that Martin Butterfield did not miss.

But Miss Gillis disappointed everybody, including Martin, who was happy to be wrong. She moved to her desk and took out her grade book, opening that terribly final document and looking at it for a moment.

"How many people would like a trip to Washington?" she suddenly asked.

As one machine, the fifth grade of Fern Township school raised its hand.

Miss Gillis smiled quickly with the optimism that was part of her nature. "Well," she said thoughtfully, "unless we do better work, I don't see how *some* people can expect to be considered in the contest."

"Some people" promptly shrank in their seats, the most noticeable shrinkage occurring in the seat occupied by Martin Butterfield.

"The next three weeks," said Miss Gillis warningly, "will decide who is the best scholar and who is the most improved scholar. It's going to be pretty nice to go to Washington . . ."

Martin Butterfield instantly had a vision of himself shaking hands with the President in front of the big dome of the Capitol—he cut the vision off before it got away with him. He had already engaged in one too many feats of the imagination this morning.

Miss Gillis peered into the grade book. Martin looked away. He wondered who had invented grade books.

"Martin," said Miss Gillis, "what grade do you expect to receive for your work in arithmetic this morning?"

It was the first time Martin had ever been asked to grade his own performance.

"Well, uh—" he said, "I don't know."

"Don't you think it ought to be zero, Martin?"

Martin listened to the titter that passed over the fifth grade. He heard Sparky Roberts distinctly . . .

"Don't you give something for keeping still?" he asked.

It was a fine stroke. Its logic and fairness appealed to the fifth grade.

Martin was greatly relieved to observe that Miss Gillis lost interest in him.

"Well," she said, "there are others here who could improve. Sparky Roberts, for instance."

Martin turned in his seat and regarded his bosom friend with the intensity of a boy studying a cooking wiener on a spit.

But Miss Gillis hurried on; she ticked off half a dozen names.

"Any one of you could win if you put yourself into it," she said with the grim and earnest hopefulness that only a young teacher is blessed with.

Martin sat up straighter yet in his seat. He could still win!

"Georgianna Semple," said Miss Gillis, "is leading for the best scholar . . ."

Martin sat so straight in his seat that his backbone ached. He *must* win!

". . . but," said Miss Gillis, "Margaret Lindsey is very close."

Martin looked around at Georgianna Semple, with the

blue eyes and golden hair. Then he cautiously turned and glared at Margaret Lindsey, with the jet black hair and dark eyes.

"Prune!" Martin muttered to himself.

Margaret Lindsey was what grown-ups term a beautifully mannered child. This term of approbation only confirmed Martin in a sober belief that she was a prune. Imagine going to Washington with her!

Miss Gillis glanced at her two prize pupils.

"Georgianna has all A's and one B for the year," she said, "and Margaret has all A's and two B's. Isn't that wonderful? Let's all give Georgianna and Margaret a big hand!"

The fifth grade applauded with the vigor that comes from a natural love of noise making and Martin Butterfield clapped in the direction of Georgianna Semple just to make his feelings clear.

After the applause, the class resumed work, and Martin Butterfield began the strenuous task of self-improvement. If he failed to make much headway that morning, he made up for it on the way home from school that afternoon.

Outside the school yard, Martin waited until Georgianna came down the walk, bearing her evening burden of books. Unfortunately, Georgianna was accompanied by that dark-haired prune, Margaret Lindsey.

Martin was very polite, however.

"Hello, Georgianna," he said. "Hi," he added, just to make it clear that his attentions were not divided evenly.

"Hello, Martin," said Georgianna.

For reasons that any female would comprehend, Margaret tossed her dark head and said nothing.

"I'll carry your books, Georgianna," Martin offered.

"You don't have to if you don't want to," Georgianna replied.

Nonetheless, Martin took over the armload while Miss

Lindsey suddenly remembered that she had to run across the street and say something to a little girl there.

"I'll see you tomorrow, Georgie," she said sweetly.

"By-by," Georgianna said even more sweetly.

Martin and Georgianna moved on in silence for a few feet.

Then Martin asked, "Why do you walk with that prune?"

Georgianna's pretty blue eyes widened.

"Martin!" she cried, "if you say things like that, you can't walk with me."

"Well," Martin said, "she *is* a—anyway, she might win your trip to Washington away from you!"

It was a telling stroke.

Georgianna's long lashes fluttered.

"Margaret is very bright and she's awfully pretty and I like her," she said with a feminine primness that was guaranteed to bring an argument, which it did.

'She's not as smart as you," Martin said vigorously. Then he paused with welling shyness. "And she ain't half as—as —well—*you* know," he finished lamely.

"Martin Butterfield, what in the world are you talking about?" Georgianna said, but she blushed prettily and Martin, deciding to abandon this little game while he was ahead, shifted subjects.

"Boy, it would certainly be swell to go to Washington," he said.

"Wouldn't it be fun to go with Miss Gillis and Margaret Lindsey?" Georgianna asked impishly.

"With Margaret!" cried Martin with pained indignation. "I wouldn't go if that pr—that girl—won the trip."

Martin's avowal of loyalty had its immediate reward.

"Would you like to start studying with me again, Martin?" asked Georgianna. "Tonight, maybe?"

Martin coughed gruffly. "Why," he said, "I guess I could —if you really wanted me to, that is . . ."

The Chart of the Improvement of Martin Butterfield seemed about to take another sharp upward turn.

Martin's resolution to improve was wonderfully strengthened by the prospect of an evening with Georgianna. Carrying his books homeward on his hip, it even seemed to him that improvement, in and of itself, was a reasonably desirable objective.

With the light of scholarship beginning to burn once again in his breast, he felt a little sorry for lesser folk in the fifth grade who did not understand the real importance of studying their lessons. He felt a distinct sense of regret for Sparky Roberts, for instance. Sparky obviously did not take his lessons seriously.

Martin was able to impart his feeling of regretful superiority to Sparky Roberts almost immediately, because that scholastically benighted soul was waiting for him in front of the Butterfield house.

"Hey, Martin," Sparky shouted, "there's a big old steam shovel digging a hole down by the state highway. Let's go down there and see what they're doing."

"A steam shovel!" Martin exclaimed before remembering that worldly pleasures come after one's duties are performed.

"What's an old steam shovel?" he added coldly.

Sparky looked suspiciously at his friend. "Are you sick or something, Martin?" he inquired, inspecting his comrade's face, nose to nose, and then scrutinizing the incriminating evidence of a large bundle of schoolbooks under arm.

"No, I'm not sick, Sparky," Martin said firmly. "It just happens I have more important stuff to do."

"Like what?" Sparky inquired.

"I've—I got to take a bath and get dressed up because I'm gonna study tonight," Martin sputtered.

If Martin had stated that he was about to dive into a pot of boiling oil, the effect could not have been more stunning.

Sparky Roberts was staggered into complete silence. Martin, fearing a recovery that would include loud, jeering noises, turned on his righteous heel and marched hastily into the safety of his own house.

It was remarkable how swiftly the study time slipped away in the Semple household.

Martin and Georgianna sat at the big dining room table while Mr. and Mrs. Semple read the papers in the parlor. The two children buzzed steadily over fractions, over the parts of speech, over the geographical features of the land of Afghanistan and over a number of other subjects which, for the last two months, had been only vague interruptions in Martin's daydreams in fifth grade.

It was amazing how much there was to know. Needless to say, the flow of help from one pupil to the other was strictly a one-way street.

"You know an awful lot," Martin kept saying.

"So will you, if you'll only pay attention," Georgianna replied.

The senior Semples, sitting in the parlor, could not but feel a certain amount of pride in a daughter who was so generous with her fellow students.

This pride was to continue for two full weeks.

Then, unfortunately, while Martin Butterfield improved to such an extent that he scored all C's in the weekly fifth-grade tests—a stupendous feat, in the view of Attorney Butterfield—there was another and less desirable result of Georgianna's tutorship.

Georgianna got a B in arithmetic while Margaret Lindsey got A's in every single thing that the fifth grade of Fern Township school offered in the way of education.

This fact not only put Margaret into a tie with Georgianna in the race for Washington, D. C., but it produced a much more acute and immediate effect.

By unanimous vote of the Semple family, not excluding its youngest member, Martin Butterfield was invited to conduct his self-improvement as best he could, without any outside assistance.

Georgianna was painfully clear on the subject. *She* waited for Martin, instead of vice versa, at the school door that fateful Friday afternoon. She had been home to lunch at noon and received some parental counsel.

She was in a state that lay halfway between womanly chagrin and womanly tears when she announced bluntly, "You can't come to my house to study any more, Martin."

Martin Butterfield was stunned. "Why not?" he asked.

Georgianna's wide blue eyes suddenly filled with tears. "You can't study with me any more," she said, " 'cause my mother says I have to teach you so hard that I can't get my own lessons done."

Because Martin was stricken speechless by this pronouncement, Georgianna went on.

"And now," she began sobbingly, "now maybe I won't win the—" but it was so awful a thought that she didn't finish it.

"You'll win, Georgianna, I know you'll win, all right," Martin said in a dismal attempt at encouragement.

"I won't either," Georgianna retorted tearfully, "and it's all your fault, Martin Butterfield!"

Martin was dazed by the enormity of what his studying at the Semple home had done.

"I'm sorry that you had to help me so much . . ." he

faltered. Then he tried again. "I didn't mean it, Georgianna," he said because he, like many another male before him, could not think of anything else to say. And, like many another luckless member of his sex, he found this explanation worth exactly nothing.

Georgianna's silent and reproachful tears rolled down her cheeks before she suddenly left him standing alone on the school ground, watching a starched and stern little feminine figure disappear rapidly down the street.

He felt impelled to run after her and tell her again that he was sorry, but he knew that it was useless. Words were not the recipe now.

Martin set out dejectedly homeward, kicking every pebble and stick on the way and rat-tatting his ruler aimlessly on every picket fence.

He took out a portion of his dismal state of mind on an unfortunate alley cat that took refuge in the upper reaches of a leafless elm. He vaguely wished that Stinker Larrabee would come home from private school so that he, Martin, could inflict some violence on a deserving person.

It wouldn't be much fun to go to Washington if Georgianna wasn't going to be there to see him shake hands with the President of the United States or somebody.

By the time Martin reached his home block, this system of reasoning had reached its logical conclusion. There would be no need to improve any more now and, though the loss of a trip to Washington was a matter not to be regarded lightly, the abandonment of the idea of going would at least permit Martin to give up the grinding work of studying every night.

This latter by-product even cheered him up a little as he entered the front door of the Butterfield house.

Mrs. Butterfield was in the kitchen, finishing the icing of a very large and very snowy coconut cake.

"This is what students who pass their examinations get," she remarked cheerfully.

"Can I have some now?" Martin inquired, moving up to the table.

"Heavens, no!" said his mother. "Supper will be ready in an hour."

No harm trying, Martin thought. He glanced again at the cake and put his books down on the nearest chair. "Has Sparky been around?" he asked.

"I haven't seen him," said Mrs. Butterfield. "He hasn't been around for a week. I wonder . . ."

"I guess he's busy," Martin said. "Maybe I'll go and see him."

Mrs. Butterfield looked up from the cake. "Now, Martin," she said, "don't you disappear just before we have supper. Remember, if you're going to study with Georgianna tonight you'll have to eat on time."

"I don't think I'll go over there tonight," Martin said cautiously.

"Why, I thought you were getting so much out of it," Mrs. Butterfield said, bending over the cake.

"Well, I can't be bothering Georgianna all the time —"

"That's true, Martin," Mrs. Butterfield said. "It might be better for you to study here by yourself. Now that you're getting along so well you can stay at home and not be troubling others."

Martin gulped. He hadn't necessarily meant he was going to study tonight.

Self-improvement, it appeared, was not a thing that the world was going to let him turn on and off, like a faucet.

"Uh-huh," he murmured.

Before his mother could pursue her point, he discovered a great need to repair to the beagle pens at the rear of the yard. Once there, he went out the back gate and down the alley where, coming from the other direction, was Sparky Roberts.

"Hi," called Martin.

"Hi yourself," replied Sparky. "I thought you'd be home doing your lessons by now."

"Who?"

"You, you bookworm!"

"Who you calling a bookworm?"

"Who do you think?"

This exchange continued for some time without any more tangible result than that both parties sat down with their backs to the fence in order to wrangle with the least possible effort.

When the argument was finally exhausted, Sparky Roberts changed the subject.

"Boy," he said with sudden warmth, "I sure wish I could get that trip to Washington."

"Why don't you study then, like I do?" Martin inquired, not seeking far for an example of what he considered good scholarship.

Sparky Roberts yipped a scoffing note that carried far up and down the alley in the quiet late afternoon.

"Georgianna's helping you," he said. "Everybody knows she is!"

The part of Martin's nature that was devoted to scholarship was perhaps small, but it was capable of being hurt out of all proportion to its size.

"I study every night," he said.

"Every night for two weeks," Sparky observed.

This shaft drove deeply into the scholarly feelings of Martin Butterfield, deeply enough perhaps to be responsible for the sudden and illuminating idea that began to take shape, with great speed, in his mind.

Martin fell silent, suddenly contemplative, and regarded

Sparky sitting beside him. Sparky began to whistle softly to himself, satisfied that he had scored another forensic victory.

When Martin spoke again, he was no more the combatant —again he was the boon friend of Sparky Roberts, his confidante and faithful comrade.

"Would you really like to go to Washington, Sparky?" he asked.

"Who wouldn't?" Sparky replied pointedly.

"Well," Martin said casually, "why don't you get somebody to help you study? That's a good way."

It was the voice of experience speaking.

Sparky paused and then gave himself to reflection.

"Would Georgianna help me, do you think?" he inquired.

"Georgianna!" cried Martin, pierced to the quick by this Benedict Arnold sort of thinking. "Why, she's my—you get somebody else."

Sparky was silenced by this imposing reaction. Martin meanwhile composed his trodden feelings sufficiently not to reveal that he, himself, had already lost the services of the most excellent young tutor in fifth grade.

He had to be careful. His plan was designed to *help* Georgianna Semple, not to destroy her scholarship completely by delivering her into the hands of another of the lesser intellectual lights of the fifth grade.

Martin looked off into the evening sky.

"Sparky," he said quietly, "why don't you ask Margaret Lindsey to help you with your lessons?"

Sparky turned and eyed Martin suspiciously.

Martin returned his gaze benignly. "She's very smart and she might do it," he added thoughtfully.

Sparky still felt a not altogether unwarranted skepticism. "You think she would?" he asked.

"You could ask her, couldn't you?" Martin inquired sarcastically. "Are you afraid of an old girl?"

Sparky was emphatically not afraid of an old girl or an old boy or any old body in the fifth grade and he made it perfectly clear, first by threatening Martin in person and then by threatening in absentia everybody in Miss Gillis' roomful of angels.

This show of force convinced Martin Butterfield that he had carried his point. He argued no more.

Sparky got up and stretched in the dusk of the alley. "Well, I guess I better be going home," he said. Then he looked down upon his companion, whose face was a study of innocence.

Sparky decided to take a necessary precaution.

"If I go and get somebody to help me study, you ain't going to go around blatting it to everybody," he announced with a nice mixture of threat and question.

"Who, me?" said Martin.

The two friends went their separate ways in the twilight shortly thereafter, one up the alley and the other down.

Right after supper Sparky phoned Martin to inform him that he, Sparky, was on his way to the Lindseys' house and Martin better not go around telling everybody.

That night the Butterfield household was treated to the spectacle of a scholar in its midst.

Martin settled down to his night's lessons with the modest hope that he had balanced certain accounts in the contest for Best Scholar of Fifth Grade. He must now make sure that the beautiful Best Scholar would have good company on her Washington excursion.

By the beginning of the week before Thanksgiving, Martin Butterfield and Sparky Roberts had become the sensations of the fifth grade of Fern Township school.

It might also be said that Martin was equally a sensation at home.

"Do you suppose there's something wrong with him, Martha?" Mr. Butterfield asked his wife one evening.

"Wrong?" murmured that good woman. "Why, he was never better—he's just been a jewel."

"That's what I mean," Mr. Butterfield said.

Martin pored over his books in the dining room, hearing every word of this conversation and pondering momentarily whether it would not be possible to derive some small advantage, financial or otherwise, from such an optimistic turn in parental opinion.

He decided to concentrate on his studies. There would be time enough for the sweet fruits of good behavior later.

Meanwhile, he must remember that Sparky Roberts, right at this moment of the evening, was over at Margaret Lindsey's house being tutored heavily.

Martin's mind came back to his arithmetic and rested there, under the stimulus of competition. His studious conduct was repeated every night right up to the Friday before Thanksgiving when the last tests would come.

When Friday morning arrived, in its slow deliberate fashion, it brought a strange experience for Martin. For the first time in his life he felt that a written examination constituted an opportunity to put on public display the extent of his knowledge, rather than a threat of the very same thing.

Remarkably, Sparky Roberts exhibited certain confident evidences of the same feeling.

"I'm just runnin' over with answers," Sparky whispered across the aisle as Miss Gillis passed out the paper.

"Don't spill 'em on the floor," Martin said sarcastically.

"Quiet now, everybody!" Miss Gillis commanded.

In a few minutes, the teacher was writing the questions

on the blackboard and the heads of the pupils were bent over their desks as they wrote the answers, or made valiant attempts.

No more valor was displayed by anyone than by Martin and Sparky, unless it was by Georgianna Semple and Margaret Lindsey in the rear, their distance from the teacher's desk being the measure of their good behavior.

The tests took an hour and when they were finished, the pupils exchanged papers. There was a brief debate involving Martin and Sparky, who mutually refused to exchange, each casting certain doubts upon the intentions of the other.

Miss Gillis interposed.

"I'll correct them both," she said briefly.

The following fifteen minutes constituted a period of utter confusion in the fifth grade.

Every answer produced some kind of question, argument or tearful rejection. It was one of those times when Miss Gillis wondered suddenly and—with a feeling of guilt—whether there was not a simpler profession than teaching school.

When the papers were corrected, Miss Gillis collected them and held a "study period" while she put the final grades on them.

Martin Butterfield turned and peered intently at Georgianna Semple. Georgianna looked away.

Martin settled gloomily in his seat. Then he turned and stared at Margaret Lindsey who was busily engaged in studying.

She *would* study after the exam, when all reason for studying had passed!

Finally Martin turned his attention to Miss Gillis, who was smiling.

Looking over the grades, Miss Gillis felt good reason for satisfaction. In all her career of teaching, extending back for one previous year, she had never seen so much improvement in a class.

Martin Butterfield had actually made a B in all his subjects in that hour-long test! And Sparky Roberts had made a C!

Of course, it was not unexpected that Georgianna Semple would make an A.

There was a faint disappointment in the marks, however. That good, studious child, Margaret Lindsey, had fallen off to a B minus. Miss Gillis could not understand that. . . .

It was just after four o'clock when Martin Butterfield and Georgianna Semple reached the front steps of the Semple house.

"I'm awful glad you won, Martin," Georgianna said.

"I'm awful glad you won, too, Georgianna," Martin replied shyly.

"I'm sorry you weren't allowed to come over and study with me last week, Martin."

"That's all right."

Georgianna's lovely face became momentarily clouded.

"I'm sorry about poor Margaret Lindsey," she said.

"Somebody has to lose," Martin remarked profoundly.

"What do you suppose happened?"

Martin knit his brows thoughtfully.

"Maybe she didn't study hard enough," he said.

Georgianna studied Martin with a minuteness that made him uncomfortable. "You mean—maybe she spent too much time helping Sparky . . ."

Martin decided to look at the good side of this picture.

"I'm glad Sparky improved as much as he did," he said generously. "He needed to improve."

Georgianna Semple's wide blue eyes looked up at Martin in mute admiration.

"You're nice, Martin," she said.

"So are you," Martin whispered.

Then he abruptly turned and fled.

Halfway down the block he looked back and she was still standing there. Martin did handsprings until he rounded the corner and passed out of her view.

He felt wonderful.

Then the Most Improved Scholar of the Fifth Grade of Fern Township school remembered it was Friday afternoon. There was no school tomorrow! All day with no lessons!

Martin made one of those loud, unintelligible, ebullient sounds with which small boys are forever puzzling grown-ups and hurried on down the street.

Saturday Postlude

Hey, Sparky!" Silence along the street under the trees in front of Sparky Roberts' house. Martin Butterfield, garbed in jeans and a khaki shirt, cupped his hands around his mouth and tried again. "Hey, Sparky!"

Still, silence.

Martin kicked impatiently at a small pebble lying on the sidewalk and momentarily considered the pebble as a more commanding method of getting attention. Here it was 7:45 A.M. on Saturday and Sparky wasn't ready. What did he think Saturday was for, anyway?

Martin cupped his hands again, drew a deep breath and was about to outdo his previous efforts when a long-barreled revolver was poked into his ribs from the Roberts hedge.

"I gotcha," said Sparky, "and don't try to get out of it. I gotcha that time."

Sparky emerged from his ambush. He, too, was in the uniform of the day, jeans and khaki shirt.

Martin Butterfield looked at his lifelong friend with complete distaste.

207

"Is that all you got to be doing?" he said. "You want me to wear my lungs out—on a Saturday?"

"What do you want to do?" Sparky inquired, retiring his monster weapon to a holster whose lanyard was tied around his thigh so low it almost reached his knee.

"I don't want to stand around hollering my head off," Martin said. "Lemme try your gun."

Sparky lifted out the big revolver.

Martin fondled it a moment with expert attention to its grip, hammer and artificial magazine. With sudden deceptiveness, he poked the revolver in Sparky's ribs.

"I got you, too," he announced calmly. "Now we're even."

"You didn't get me as good as I got you, though," Sparky replied. "I gave you the gun."

"It counts, anyway," Martin said, dismissing the whole subject. "Now let's do something. You'd think every day was Saturday the way you fool around."

The two friends gravitated toward the curb and sat down under the trees.

"It sure is nice to have a day off," Sparky said. "You don't know what a day off is till you go to school all week."

"Sometimes a week seems like a year," Martin replied.

The boys sat on the curb and stared out into the street, reflecting moodily on the length of a week and the brevity of a Saturday.

"Wouldn't it be great if every day was Saturday?" Martin asked.

"What'd you do with all the Sundays that came right afterwards?" Sparky inquired.

"I was just pretending," Martin retorted. "Can't you pretend anything, Sparky, without getting all mixed up?"

Sparky was looking down the street.

"I can pretend I see some old farmer driving his horses," he announced. "Look down there!"

He pointed.

Two or three blocks away, a pair of heavy farm horses plodded toward the boys on the curb. The team of bays was hauling a light wagon and the figure of the farmer rode high above them on the wagon seat.

Martin and Sparky watched the horses, whose heads nodded heavily as they picked up their big hocks one after another and made a solid clopping sound on the pavement, amid soft creakings of leather and harness.

"Wonder where they're going?" Sparky asked.

The horses and wagon came closer and the rolling wheels made a soft rumbling sound on the early morning air.

"Probably awful far or they wouldn't start so early," said Martin.

"I'd sure like to have a team of old horses and sit up there on the seat and drive them like this . . ." Sparky said.

He sat up straight on the curb and held out his arms as if he were handling the jerkline on a team of four hauling a Wells-Fargo express coach.

Both boys sat immobile as the wagon came on.

They cupped their chins in their hands and studied the leisurely, powerful motion of the big horses and the careless air of the farmer slumped round-shouldered above his chargers; they imagined themselves up there in the driver's place on a Saturday morning when the sun was shining, the day was new and every point of the compass beckoned with half-whispered promises of adventure such as no boy ever had before.

The wagon and the horses rolled up even with the boys' place on the curb.

It was then that Martin and Sparky recognized that the

driver on the seat was blissfully dozing while his horses knowledgeably hauled him to whatever destination was mutually theirs.

Martin drank in this godsend of a sleeping driver.

"What do you say, Sparky?" he asked as the wagon rolled past to reveal that its tail gate was half-down and its bed full of new yellow straw.

"If he's asleep he won't care," said Sparky.

Martin and Sparky, one moment sitting on the curbstone with their chins in their hands, were the next moment running like silent, alert rabbits.

With an easy spring they heaved themselves up on the tail gate of the slowly rolling wagon, twisting in mid-air to land expertly on their pants seats.

With their feet dangling, they rolled away into the long, pure, perfectly unpredictable pleasures of Saturday, a day that was put into the calendar for small boys alone.